CANDLELIGHT REGENCY SPECIAL

CANDLELIGHT REGENCIES

245   LA CASA DORADA, *Janet Louise Roberts*
246   THE GOLDEN THISTLE, *Janet Louise Roberts*
247   THE FIRST WALTZ, *Janet Louise Roberts*
248   THE CARDROSS LUCK, *Janet Louise Roberts*
250   THE LADY ROTHSCHILD, *Samantha Lester*
251   BRIDE OF CHANCE, *Lucy Phillips Stewart*
253   THE IMPOSSIBLE WARD, *Dorothy Mack*
255   THE BAD BARON'S DAUGHTER, *Laura London*
257   THE CHEVALIER'S LADY, *Betty Hale Hyatt*
263   MOONLIGHT MIST, *Laura London*
501   THE SCANDALOUS SEASON, *Nina Pykare*
505   THE BARTERED BRIDE, *Anne Hillary*
512   BRIDE OF TORQUAY, *Lucy Phillips Stewart*
515   MANNER OF A LADY, *Cilla Whitmore*
521   LOVE'S CAPTIVE, *Samantha Lester*
527   KITTY, *Jennie Tremaine*
530   BRIDE OF A STRANGER, *Lucy Phillips Stewart*
537   HIS LORDSHIP'S LANDLADY, *Cilla Whitmore*
542   DAISY, *Jennie Tremaine*
543   THE SLEEPING HEIRESS, *Phyllis Taylor Pianka*
548   LOVE IN DISGUISE, *Nina Pykare*
549   THE RUNAWAY HEIRESS, *Lillian Cheatham*
554   A MAN OF HER CHOOSING, *Nina Pykare*
555   PASSING FANCY, *Mary Linn Roby*
562   LUCY, *Jennie Tremaine*
563   PIPPA, *Megan O'Connor*
570   THOMASINA, *Joan Vincent*
571   SENSIBLE CECILY, *Margaret Summerville*
572   DOUBLE FOLLY, *Julia Anders*
573   POLLY, *Jennie Tremaine*
578   THE MISMATCHED LOVERS, *Anne Hillary*
579   UNWILLING BRIDE, *Julia Anders*
580   INFAMOUS ISABELLE, *Margaret Summerville*
581   THE DAZZLED HEART, *Nina Pykare*
586   THE EDUCATION OF JOANNE, *Joan Vincent*
587   MOLLY, *Jennie Tremaine*
588   JESSICA WINDOM, *Marnie Ellingson*
589   THE ARDENT SUITOR, *Marian Lorraine*
593   THE RAKE'S COMPANION, *Regina Towers*
594   LADY INCOGNITA, *Nina Pykare*
595   A BOND OF HONOR, *Joan Vincent*
596   GINNY, *Jennie Tremaine*
597   THE MARRIAGE AGREEMENT, *Margaret MacWilliams*

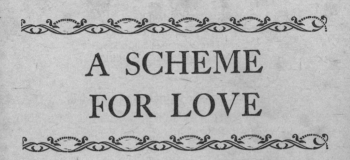

A SCHEME
FOR LOVE

Joan Vincent

A CANDLELIGHT REGENCY SPECIAL

Published by
Dell Publishing Co., Inc.
1 Dag Hammarskjold Plaza
New York, New York 10017

To Mom
who was the instrument of my being;

To Mrs. C.
who fostered it;

To Vera
whose gift inspired this tale of
a "widow in black, doll in red."

Dell ® TM 681510, Dell Publishing Co., Inc.

ISBN 0-440-18387-1

Printed in the United States of America

First printing—September 1980

CHAPTER ONE

February, 1802. The Treaty of Amiens was about to be concluded, bringing respite from the long years of war with France for the people of Britain. Soon rejoicing would break over the land in surging waves. But in the town of Horley, in the shire of Surrey, at the home of Sir Howard Bartone, neither war nor peace intruded. In this one small part of the island nation a hopeless battle had been waged and was now drawing to its end.

Shrouding curtains concealed bright sun from the sombre chamber. The ancient fourposter bore its unstirring inhabitant in the puffed splendour of satin pillows and rich woolen blankets.

The wan figure of the old man looked as if it was about to be swallowed by the bolsters heaped about him. To one side a young woman sat in a pose of quiet waiting. At the foot of the bed stood a middle-aged man of grave countenance.

Hearing a sound, Mathilda raised her eyes to

stare at the man in the bed, then sighed as she saw he remained the same. She could feel no grief as she awaited his dying, for she longed for death to release him.

Suddenly his eyes, like shutters thrown open to the light of day, flared apart to reveal a stark gaze. The lips trembled as they tried to speak. Mathilda rose and leaned toward him.

"Tillie," the feeble voice managed, "Tillie, think not too harshly of me. 'Tis you I was thinking of. But . . . now . . ." strength failed, and the barely audible whisper was hushed to stillness.

"Do not disturb yourself, Bartone," she said awkwardly, to reassure him. In his eyes she read a different stress, one not caused by pain, and knew not what to do. "Is there someone you wish me to summon?" she asked, uncertainty bringing wrinkles of concern to her smooth, round face.

"I fear . . . I fear have . . . been unwise . . . but it was done for the best," the old man said with laboured breath.

"Of course, Bartone, of course," she crooned as to a child. Kneeling beside the bed, she took his cold hand into her warm ones.

A hand's firm grip closed on her shoulder. "It is near," Dr. Bolen said quietly as he stood at her side.

The old man's eyes widened momentarily; his fingers worked to clutch Mathilda's. A plea—was it for forgiveness?—contorted his features until a soft sigh sounded and his face relaxed into the empty expression of death.

Mathilda continued to gaze at him as the doctor reached past her and closed the unseeing eyes. "He rests at last," she said tiredly.

"And now you must," Dr. Bolen urged, taking the withered hand from hers and laying it across the old man's sunken chest. He placed a hand beneath her arm and helped her rise. "You really must rest. There will be the funeral to be got through."

"Yes," she returned vacantly.

"Is there someone I can send for to stay with you during these first days?" the doctor asked, thinking how helpless the young woman looked. Why Bartone had ever decided to marry such a one as she so late in his years he could never guess. But the young woman had been kind and gentle. Her care during this last illness had never ceased, nor had she complained. The doctor started, realizing Lady Bartone was staring at him.

"Yes, madam?"

"What was it you asked of me?" she repeated.

"Asked? Oh, is there someone who can come and stay with you for a few weeks?"

"Come?" Mathilda shrugged. "Why, no one. I am quite alone in the world. Mother passed away the same year Sir Bartone and I were wed. There was no one else. Mr. Petersbye, the solicitor, said he would see to all the proper notifications when the time came."

"Then I shall stop by his home and apprise him of the turn here."

"I suppose that will do. . . . Yes, thank you. But—" she hesitated, turning to look back at the huge bed.

"Dannon will know what to do," the doctor assured her. Opening the outer door of the bed-chamber, he glanced over the small group await-ing them and announced, "Your master has passed to his reward."

The tall, slightly bent figure of the aged butler, Dannon, sagged as if a great weight had been placed upon his shoulders. A sob, smothered by the great white apron held to her mouth, escaped from the housekeeper, Dannon's wife, affection-ately called Mrs. Bertie.

Sal, the simple-minded scullery maid, and Old Jerry, the last of the once numerous grooms, made up the remainder of the group.

"I am sorry, Dannon," Mathilda said, knowing the affection the old retainer had for his master. "He died peacefully—his pain relieved at last," she assured them all.

"See that your mistress rests," Dr. Bolen or-dered Mrs. Bertie. "Dannon, see to Sir Bartone's last needs."

"Don't worry now, Doctor, I'll see to her," Mrs.

Bertie said, wrapping a motherly arm about her young mistress.

"All will be as he would wish, madam," Dannon assured her.

"Oh, milady!" wailed Sal, "What'll become of us?" She moaned and raised her hands in an exaggerated pose of fear.

"Stop your silly chatter, and fetch some warm water for the mistress," Mrs. Bertie reproved the girl sharply.

"You may call upon me for whatever the need," Dr. Bolen said to Mathilda, bowing slightly. "My condolences, of course," he added in farewell.

The departing echo of the doctor's steps fell silent as Mrs. Bertie turned in the direction of Mathilda's room. "Best be to your room, miss," she said, and nodded to Dannon to enter the master's chamber.

The old butler's movement drew Mathilda's frozen attention away from Sal at last.

"I said fetch water," Mrs. Bertie scolded, "and it had better be warm or your backside will be," she called after the girl.

Propelled forward by the housekeeper, Mathilda slipped into reverie. It had been just six weeks since Bartone had fallen ill. Six weeks that she had spent almost entirely in the sickroom. That had been, after all, her bargain—a home in exchange for companionship and care; a home and care for her sick mother. She had no regrets about striking the agreement. Long before Bartone had approached her with his own offer, she had accepted the fact that there was neither home nor husband for her.

"Why don't you lie down, miss?" Mrs. Bertie said, interrupting her thoughts. "I'll see to something for you to eat. No need for you to waste away nor make yourself ill. Heaven knows you'll need your strength now."

Something in the housekeeper's tone caught Mathilda's attention. A questioning look brought no answer, only a pat on the hand before the woman swung her heavy form out of the room.

As the door closed, the small portrait of Mathilda's mother hanging near it brought fresh memories of her wedding day, little more than three years ago. The small bust portrait had been Bartone's gift to her their first Michaelmas together.

Together. The word came back in heckling ripples. Mathilda lifted her chin proudly—she was not ashamed of their pact. It had served them both well—he, a lonely old man needing care, companionship; she, a spinster with an ailing mother, without funds or prospects. Some would term their marriage a mockery, the relationship of a grandfather to a granddaughter, but its form had been needed to grant respectability to their common residence.

Yes, she thought, there were many who thought Sir Bartone daft to marry the daughter of a clergyman who had pursued the way of the Lord so thoroughly he had left his family destitute of worldly means.

Even Dannon and Mrs. Bertie had treated her as a scheming tart for the first six months she had lived at Bartone Hollows, and Mrs. Bertie still called her "Miss," although Mathilda knew that was from habit now. Mathilda's position in Horley before her marriage had been that of a charity case. Living off the parish and suffering ill treatment by the well-to-do had toughened her for the snubs and snide remarks the "proper" women dealt her after her marriage. She knew they would make the funeral a terribly bleak and lonely affair. Even Bartone's two sisters, the only survivors of seven children, had made no response to her letters advising them of his illness.

A tired sigh escaped her as she undid her bodice and began to undress. The chill of the room kept her near the fireplace, where a small fire struggled to keep its life. In only a chemise and petticoats, Mathilda wrapped a woolen shawl about her closely. Squatting, she lay a log upon the bed of dim coals from which a weak flame flickered here and there. With a crackling ferociousness, flames spurted anew, enveloping the dry wood and pushing forth warmth. She watched the flames with dry eyes, their hazel colouring darkening. Her gnawing sorrow was not from loss of love but from regret that all must grow old and pass away.

Bartone's life had been long, and he had thought it full. She was happy to have lightened his last years. Now her part of the bargain was at end; she had met all terms, and he had promised she would have no care for the future.

With that thought, Mathilda rose. "Then, why . . ." she began aloud, then paused. Why? The word echoed ominously. Why Bartone's strange look as if to beg forgiveness? Why Sal's words, poor simple Sal, who could not know of their arrangement. Why Mrs. Bertie's strange aside? Why did they all frighten her so?

"My lord! My lord, welcome home!" Green greeted Viscount William Michael Maine Bartone as he signaled the footmen to remove his lordship's luggage from the post-chaise. "We did not expect you this soon," he continued as he followed the viscount's brisk steps into the family's London residence just off Piccadilly.

"We had a fair wind," came the strong-voiced reply, as the young man glanced into the receiving salon before walking on.

The elderly butler managed to reach the viscount's side and was reaching for the caped coat when the young man hurried toward his late father's office.

Green shook his head as he followed. Time for

me to retire, he thought, if I cannot manage to get milord's coat and gloves in the hall. He picked up these items from where his lordship had carelessly tossed them—a chair to one side of the office doors.

"What is this?" came the annoyed question as the viscount studied a battered trunk resting upon the rug beside his desk.

"We do not know, my lord. It arrived a fortnight ago. There was the question of what to do with it, and as you were expected soon, it was thought best to leave it here till your arrival."

"Why didn't Lynn see to it? Has he been shirking matters since my father's death?"

"No, my lord. Of course not. He may have wished for your return earlier—it having been nigh to ten and eight months since his lordship's death," Green dared, "but he would never shirk a duty," he ended, as if his own reputation had been assaulted.

"Easy, man, I simply wish to know why this decrepit item has been left to languish here instead of being placed in the garbage where it belongs," the viscount said with the disarming smile that had eased many an affront.

"There is a letter—it came the same time as the trunk. Yes, I do believe they were delivered at the same time. It is lying on your desk, my lord, and should explain the matter. The trunk was brought from Horley, in Surrey, and the instructions sent with it by a Sir Howard Bartone stated that no one should give further orders as to its disposition until you, and only you, had read the letter."

"Sir Howard Bartone?"

"I believe he was of the lineage of a brother to your great-great-grandfather, the first viscount. You may recall a Lady Pennypiece, who called upon your father from time to time—I believe she was Sir Bartone's sister."

"I do not, Green, but then I have been gone for many years." He cocked his head in thought. "Is there reason you think I should recall her?"

"She was the lady"—Green's eyes rolled slightly—"who, my lord, had the habit of using a bird's nest to adorn her coiffure. Your father was rather fond of recalling how it fell into the then Admiral Jervis's soup one night at dinner."

A broad smile came with the remembrance. "I recall the tale—how St. Vincent looked to his soup and ate as if the nasty thing wasn't there. Then Lady Pennypiece chanced to see it, felt her massive powdered dome, and reached across the table to pluck it from his bowl and place it back upon her head," Bartone said, as he went through the motions of the scene. He chuckled as he remembered how his father had acted the scene out for the family. "But that was many years ago and she was already an old woman."

"I believe she survives to this day, my lord. In fact she has a son near your age. However, Sir

Bartone passed away a week past. The notice was in the *Gazette*."

"If he is no longer, the trunk cannot be important. Have it taken to the attics. I will see to the letter later. This is my first day back in London and I do not intend to become closeted with Lynn. There is just one meeting I must be off to as soon as I refresh myself, but I have plans for this eve. We shall dine here, I believe. Send my card to Lord Potters and have him come round. What time would you suggest, Green? I know little of the ways here."

"Eight, my lord, or even nine would do."

"By Napoleon's bootstraps," ejaculated the viscount. "I can see I have much to grow accustomed to."

"Do you wish me to help you dress, my lord?" Green asked, as his lordship made for the doors.

"No, I am much accustomed to doing for myself. See to that trunk—now."

CHAPTER TWO

"So you saw St. Vincent this afternoon?" Lord Potters asked Viscount Bartone as the two enjoyed their after-dinner port.

"Yes, he wanted to reminisce about his West Indies years and to know how things now stood."

"And?"

"Potters, you surprise me. Interested in politics? I thought the demimonde held your thoughts entirely," teased Bartone.

"Have to take some interest since I came to my seat," the thin, bespectacled figure returned huffily. "I only meant to inquire about your plantations or whatever you call them."

"All is well enough for me. If peace holds, as St. Vincent thinks it will, we may all become richer. You should come with me when I return. It would give you some colour. You're like a ghost, man."

"I'd rather not be taken for an Indian, as you will be," Potters said, his narrow gaze concentrating on Bartone's deeply tanned complexion. "Although the ladies will all be agog at you, I dare say," he added. "But I thought it was your intent to remain in London, at least in England, and see to your father's holdings."

Bartone finished his port and rose. "I am undecided. Perhaps you can show me a reason to remain. Our capes," he ordered Green. "Where do you suggest we go for the finest in English womanhood?" he asked Potters.

"My mother speaks highly of Almack's, but one has to be approved to enter there, so it is out until you can call on Lady Jersey, although I rather think the Princess Levien is more to your taste. Let us stop at my quarters and see if there are any cards for soirees this eve."

"Now who is the tease?" Bartone remarked. "The flowers of womanhood I wish to meet would never be at Almack's or your dull soirees. Let us go to White's, and fortune will lead us from there."

". . . and thus it is my wish that my wife, Mathilda Bartone, be given the period of one year from the day of my death in which to locate the heretofore described object known as Doll in Red and hand it over to my solicitor, Mr. Petersbye. If she is unsuccessful, my material possessions and all funds shall go to Viscount William Bartone." The parchment crackled in the stunned silence as the solicitor rolled the document. "You understand, Lady Bartone, that I advised his lordship against this scheme, but he was set upon it.

"He set aside an allowance of five hundred pounds for your use during the remainder of your year," Mr. Petersbye added, hoping to lighten the dismay he saw on her ladyship's face.

"There is no more? No mention is made of Dannon or Mrs. Bertie?" she asked, still absorbing what she had heard.

"Sir Bartone indicated he would leave their care to your discretion. I believe his words were—if you will forgive the familiarity—'Tillie is a generous soul. She'll see them well taken care of.'" The solicitor stood, shuffling the few documents he had taken from the folio upon his desk into neat order. His uneasy glance at the widow before him was not without pity, but there was nothing he could do, as he believed Bartone was in sound mind at the time the will was drawn up. It was his fond hope the lady would not fly into whoops. "Is your man awaiting you?" he asked, as she made no move to rise.

Realizing she had been dismissed, Mathilda rose hurriedly. "Yes, he is. Oh . . . well, thank you, Mr. Petersbye."

"Keep in mind that you can draw upon your husband's estate for the five hundred pounds," the solicitor repeated as he escorted her to the door. "Good day."

"Good day to you," Mathilda repeated from

habit. She still could not believe it was true, that impossible condition set to her inheritance. She could never fulfill it. The most condemning aspect, to her mind, was Bartone's neglect of Dannon, Mrs. Bertie, and Old Jerry. She had given him only a few years; they had worked a lifetime. A widow only three weeks and already penniless, Mathilda thought. Well, not quite. There is the five hundred pounds. I could take it and leave Horley. Perhaps start a school or . . . No.

Bartone had, unfortunately for her, been all too correct in thinking she would care for the servants. The five hundred pounds would have to serve all. Sal could find other work, but the Dannons and Old Jerry were far too old to be taken on by anyone. Bartone had never mentioned this viscount, nor had the others spoken of him, so there was no reason to suppose he would give them a yearly stipend. What was she to do?

Old Jerry hobbled from the head of the team to the ancient Berlin's side, opened the door, fumbled the steps into place, and held out his hand to assist her in. The coach had been broken out especially for this occasion; after many years of disuse it was in sad disrepair. Before she took Old Jerry's hand, Mathilda swung her eyes over the swaybacked team, age showing in their every line. Managing a smile to show her appreciation of his efforts, she stepped into the motheaten interior.

Once luxurious and plush, the cloth covering the seat was threadbare and frayed. The groom's attempts to brush a semblance of neatness into it had caused further damage; tuffs of horsehair stood through slits in the rotted elegance.

An old style, the Berlin was completely unsprung, and the brief ride back to Bartone Hollows on the outskirts of Horley was enough to convince Mathilda that the coach must be forever consigned to storage. She had consented to its use this time only because Old Jerry's rheumatism would have been unduly aggravated if he had had to change the team to the improvised landaulet she customarily drove herself. Why the old groom had taken on the painful and strenuous task of readying the ancient Berlin for today's visit she did not know; she could only attribute it to his wanting to show all that Sir Bartone's widow was to receive due respect. The gesture warmed her heart and added weight to her thought that the major part of the five hundred pounds must go to the three who had served Bartone for most of their lives.

Back at Bartone Hollows, Dannon helped Mathilda from the coach, scrutinizing her closely.

"Old Jerry, please come to the library when you have finished with the horses. Dannon, I would appreciate it if you and Mrs. Bertie would come also. I shall be there as soon as I change."

"As you wish, madam," Dannon answered stiffly, as he nodded meaningfully at Old Jerry.

"And, Old Jerry . . . thank you . . . for . . . the coach." Mathilda turned quickly and dashed up the steps. Dannon would be most upset if she surrendered to the tears which threatened, she told herself. One must always be an example to the servants, she could almost hear Bartone saying.

Once changed from the black silk, which Bartone had insisted she have made when her mother had died, to the black bombazine daydress she had made herself, Mathilda felt more in control. She was uncertain what to say to the three servants but determined to take the worst of this blow upon herself. Being young and more accustomed to frugality than to frippery, she would manage.

A slight cough turned her head. The three stood before her. From their expressions she had the uneasy feeling they knew what the solicitor had told her.

"As you know," she began weakly, "I saw Mr. Petersbye this morn." Mathilda laughed shakily. "Of course, you know that."

No smile answered her from the three servants.

"He told me that Sir Bartone had altered his will not more than six months past. A condition for my inheriting anything from his estate has been set and—" She tried to look them directly in the eye but failed. "And there is no mention in the will of any of you."

As she had expected, no gasp, not a sound came from the three. Slowly she raised her gaze. They stood still, stiffly at attention, their faces blank.

"Provision has been made for a sum of money for my use during the next year. I mean to divide it—the greater part of it—between you and will do what I can to see you suitably settled before I depart," she hurried to add.

"You be leaving?" Old Jerry asked oddly.

"We can only take our due wages," Dannon said coldly.

"Aren't you even going to try for it?" Mrs. Bertie blurted out.

"Mum, be still," Dannon corrected her.

"No, wait," Mathilda ordered. "Do you know about the stipulation of the will? Answer me."

Guilt crept over all three, and Dannon murmured ascent.

"How long have you known?"

"If truth must be told, madam, we've known it since the day the new will was drawn," Dannon explained. "Mr. Petersbye called here on the day of the week that you make your rounds of the parish cases; I was sent for the portrait and happened to overhear a little. Knowing his lordship, I found it not hard to guess what he had done."

"Why didn't you tell me? Perhaps I could have prevented all this."

"His lordship was not known for altering his decisions, madam."

"You must try and find her, miss," urged Mrs. Bertie. "You must. For yourself as well as for us. His lordship would never have set such a condition on the inheritance if it didn't mean more than it appears. He always had reasons for his doings."

"I would not know where to begin. Why, the description of the doll is vague. I can't even think what she must look like," Mathilda protested.

"There's a remedy for that," the housekeeper said happily. "Dannon, go fetch the portrait."

"Even if you do have a resemblance of her, where is the search to begin? We have been through most of the rooms of the house since I came, cleaning and setting them aright, and I saw nothing that resembled a doll."

"Here it is, madam," Dannon said as he reentered the library. "Where shall I set it?"

"There." Mathilda pointed to a side table. "Lean it there, where the light from the window is good."

Standing the portrait against the table, Dannon stepped back, keeping himself aloof as the other two crowded beside Mathilda to look at the portrait.

"Is this Sir Bartone's family?" Mathilda asked as she gazed at the family setting. "Which is he?"

"I believe the one standing before Mrs. Bartone," Dannon answered.

"But look, miss. Look at the little girl sitting on the carpet. See the doll she holds, with its fine red gown. Even a hat and a parasol it has. That is Doll in Red."

CHAPTER THREE

Rotten Row was crowded with high-perch phaetons, barouches, and mounted riders, all enjoying the afternoon promenade in the warmth of early April. Dandies, ladies, beaux, and the best of the demimonde vied with each other in elegance of dress and quality of horseflesh. The Duchess of Devonshire, the Dukes royal, Beau Brummel and his friends, Lord Avanley and Apsely were among those enjoying the warm sun and the hotter quips of their companions in judgment of the dress and style of those wishing to join the *ton*.

One figure they had noted and commented favourably upon was mounted atop a prime-blooded chestnut stallion. From boot to hat the soft fawn hues that graced the lean, young form of Viscount Bartone offset his dark locks and tanned complexion admirably. It was not only the social arbiters who smiled and nodded as he passed but also many of Harriet Wilson's mold, who had become well acquainted with the young lord during his month in London. All, especially the ladies of the *beau monde*, found the viscount's evasive behaviour challenging.

"Least you could do is nod," Lord Potters muttered to his friend. "It's beyond me why I must come with you when a scowl is all you deal anyone. Embarrassing it is and—" Potters's words ended abruptly as his mount shied at a carriage, nearly causing his lordship to lose his seat as he jerked on the reins.

"I cannot fathom why you are still such an abominable horseman," Bartone drawled, the edge in his voice indicating his annoyance.

"You know the beasts dislike me," snapped his bespectacled friend, shifting uneasily in the saddle. "I told you, the only civilized way to do this was in my phaeton."

"Risking my life against the French, against pirateers, even against rebellious natives is more to my liking than riding in a phaeton you choose to drive," the viscount said drily.

Potters adjusted his spectacles agitatedly, a sure sign offense had been taken.

"I would ride in your landau," Bartone offered.

"Only because I do not drive it," Potters snapped. Pointedly looking away, he nodded at a pair of ladies passing close by. When the two men were again apart from the bustle, Potters continued. "What is it you wish of me, Will? Neither my riding nor my driving pleases you. I cannot begin to be even a two-bottle man. You are bored with anything that pleases me and insist upon dragging me to those gaming hells. Gambling, drinking—that is not enough, we have to squire those light-skirts about." He wrinkled his nose in distaste.

A bark of laughter answered him. "You must be the only man in England who has not succumbed to the pleasures of life. Are you becoming a Methodist?" Bartone asked sardonically. He glanced away, then looked back, regret playing over his features. "I do try you fretfully."

"If only I knew what it is you are trying to find. What are you to gain from this fast pace toward nothing?"

An indolent shrug was his answer.

"I am only good enough to see you safely home when you're in your cups," Potters said quietly.

"You know better than that. We've been friends since childhood."

"I wonder. Sometimes I think I'm merely someone who amuses you, someone it pleases you to lead about and make a fool of."

"That is not what I mean to do. Who knows why I . . . Something is missing and I can't determine what. I'm bored with the whole bloody business."

"Why don't you get involved—take on responsibility? I'd wager a hundred pounds that you have spent fewer than five hours with your man Lynn since you arrived."

"I won't become like y—"

"Like me? Yes. That is exactly what you need."

"I need a hard gallop, not this lazy pace," Bartone quipped, and laid his whip to his mount.

Shaking his head as he watched riders and carriages swerve out of the viscount's way, Potters muttered, "I hope I survive until you find whatever it is you're searching for."

Smudges of dust and swatches of spider webs covered the four searchers working through the old trunks, wooden boxes, and heaps of discarded household goods in the far west attic corner of Bartone Hollows. One by one, with either a gesture or look of futility, they halted their rummaging. Mrs. Bertie was the last to quit and then only when urged to do so by the others.

"It is no use," Mathilda said tiredly. "Unless there is some hidden chamber or secret vault, the doll cannot be in this house."

"There are none of those, madame," Dannon told her. "Sir Bartone and I were children when this house was built, and we came with his father whenever he inspected the builders' progress. Why, we scampered and crawled over every inch. In later years, when Sir Bartone did renovations, I worked with him and viewed the house plans. No, we have searched every possibility here."

"We did our best," Mathilda noted, trying to put a cheery resolve into her voice for the sake of the others. "Now we must plan for the future, for we know what it brings. Let us go freshen up." She led the way toward the door, halting by it when she realized none of the others had followed. Looking back in the dim light given off by the candles they had brought with them, she saw the three hunched over something. While Mathilda watched, they straightened, spoke briefly among themselves, and then turned to face her.

"What is it?" she asked. "Did you find it?"

"No, miss," Mrs. Bertie answered, "but Dannon recalled that this chest"—she motioned to the smallish wooden box they had been bending over—"belonged to Miss Bartone—the Miss Bartone holding the doll in the family portrait."

"I do not see what that can mean to us if the doll is not in the chest," Mathilda stated brusquely. "Let us get into the light and out of this dusty place."

"Of course, madame," Dannon said before Mrs. Bertie could speak. "I shall see that some warm water is brought to your chamber."

"Thank you, Dannon. I shall dine as usual."

"Yes, madame." He bowed and signaled the other two to be silent as the mistress left them.

"Now, why did you do that, Dannon?" scolded Mrs. Bertie.

"Ye could have let us ask—ye agreed to it," huffed Old Jerry.

"Madame was tired—could you not see that?" he defended himself.

The other two nodded, quieted by his words.

"When she is rested and has eaten, she will be much more inclined to agree to our plan," Dannon continued with assurance.

"It does seem a shame to use the young miss so," Mrs. Bertie murmured.

"Aye, she has been nothing but kindness to us and means to share the funds," Old Jerry offered.

Dannon straightened himself and looked squarely at his wife. "It was you who said the master always had his reasons for his doings. He wanted madame to search for the doll, and our duty lies in seeing his will done. We cannot search elsewhere for it; only madame can do that. It's not as if she will not gain from it. Do you want to see Lady Bartone a parish case? I, for one, have served this proud name too long to see such happen if it can be helped," he finished with an abrupt nod.

"Aye," responded Old Jerry with renewed enthusiasm.

Mrs. Bertie patted her husband's thin back. "I told me mum you would always be the best," she said with a tear in her eye. "Let's see to that water and a fitting meal for the mistress."

"Tell Mrs. Bertie that the meal was excellent," Mathilda instructed Dannon as she rose from her solitary feast of roasted veal garnished with succulent carrots and scallops, spiced pears, and delicate sweets. "I shall retire now."

"Madam, could we speak with you before you do so?" Dannon requested.

"Of course." Mathilda brightened, happy to be spared another lonely eve in her room.

"I have had a fire laid in the morning room," the butler said with a bow.

"That will be fine, Dannon. I will go there now."

The morning room was one of the smaller rooms of the house, and the well-laid fire had given it a cozy warmth. Mathilda seated herself and pondered the odd relationship that now existed between herself and the old retainers.

They were more friends than servants, and yet they refused to eat with her, or to visit, deeming it improper. Unknowingly, at least unthinkingly, they thus condemned her to unbroken loneliness. Mathilda had been proven sadly correct about the people of Horley. Many came to the funeral, but she did not know whether it was to pay respects to Sir Bartone or to deal her an outright snub. Not a soul had spoken to her then and none had called at Bartone Hollows since that day. March had ended and so had any hope Mathilda had cosseted for finding Doll in Red.

Dannon entered with his usual stateliness, the other two following.

Mathilda had a thought to ask them to sit but discarded it immediately, knowing their usual reply. "What is it you wish?" she asked.

"There is an idea, miss, that we've come upon," Mrs. Bertie began. "It's about the doll."

"You know we have searched every possible area," interrupted Mathilda.

"Pardon, madam," Dannon broke in. "We have searched every place *here*, at Bartone Hollows."

"Here?"

"Yes, miss," Mrs. Bertie went on excitedly. "Dannon has looked in the registry and found that Miss Bartone has married a Squire Pellum and that they live near Farnham. Now, we was thinking you could go and call on Mrs. Pellum and ask about the doll."

"What my wife means," Dannon said, "is that it would be most fitting for you to travel to Farnham, taking the small chest of childhood mementos we discovered today. It would be quite natural for you to mention the portrait and to ask, indirectly of course, about the doll."

"But I have never met Mrs. Pellum, nor have I ever traveled except as a young child," objected Mathilda.

"I am somewhat knowledgeable in matters of travel," said Dannon. "Lord Chatham frequently required Sir Bartone in London years ago and I always arranged matters. You would have to go on the mailcoach, however, Sir Bartone's team and equipage being rather . . ."

"That would not trouble me, I think," Mathilda said hesitantly. "But would this be wise? No one knows of my predicament, and I do not think any of Sir Bartone's relatives would be inclined to aid me," she told them matter-of-factly.

The three were forced to acknowledge the truth of her words.

"But you wouldn't need to tell them you were searching for the doll—only ask questions, well, in . . . in a . . ."

"I think I know what you mean, Mrs. Bertie," smiled Mathilda, "but there will be expenses involved in such an undertaking, and any amount used will only decrease what I have to give you."

"We understand that," Dannon said, "and still wish you to make the effort."

Mathilda studied each one. Finally, she sighed. "As you wish, although I stress that I feel there is naught to be gained."

"I will make the arrangements in the morn, madam. Perhaps there is a coach leaving then that you can take. Mrs. Bertie will pack for you. And . . . thank you, madam," Dannon finished stiffly. The men bowed, Mrs. Bertie gave her impression of a curtsy, and they left their mistress sitting alone once more.

"Now what have you got yourself into," Mathilda murmured aloud. "A journey . . . no, an adventure," she said sitting upright. "I do believe I understand why Bartone put that stipulation in the will. He wished to give me some adventure. Why, I recall how he once said it was sadly lacking for me here." She settled back, thinking. The doll is probably there awaiting me; yes, that is it, she thought happily, now eagerly looking forward to the journey.

A rough shake brought Lord Potters to awareness of the day. Lifting his nightcap off one eye, which he opened warily, he saw Viscount Bartone's beaming smile.

"Oh, 'tis you," he muttered, pulling the nightcap tightly down and tugging the pillow over his head.

"Come, Potts, arise. I am taking your advice."

"My advice is for you to return home and go back to bed."

"I was as late to mine as you, old man," Bartone countered. "As a matter of fact, I tucked you in this time."

"Go away."

"Here I am, come to reform, and all you can do is hide your head," Bartone said accusingly.

"Reform? You?" came skeptically from beneath the pillow. Slowly the figure sat and fumbled for his spectacles on the bedside table. Adjusting them, Potters stared at his friend. "It is barely noon," he said, shifting his vision to the clock on the mantel. "You have gone mad at last."

"Surely you recall the other day in the park? You told me I must assume some responsibility. I have decided to take your advice. We leave for Horley as soon as you dress."

"We? There is nothing in my suggestion that says I need more responsibility, and what does Horley or whatever have to do with either of us? Besides," he rushed on, "I promised Mother I would escort her to the opera this eve."

"You won't fob me off that easily," Bartone laughed, and pulled off the bedcovers. Giving the bell cord a pull, he said, "I'll sample the breakfast fare below while you manage your toilet."

A short time later a scowling figure joined the viscount in the breakfast room.

"Time for tea and a bite or two," the viscount greeted Lord Potters. "Don't wish to have my man handle the team any longer than necessary."

"Now listen, I am not going with you to Hoathly—whatever," Potters stated firmly.

"I said Horley. A cousin of mine passed away there not long ago. It's in Surrey. Before he died he sent a rather curious old trunk to me. I couldn't locate the letter that came with it when I looked for it this morn. Lynn must have put it somewhere for safekeeping and I must see him about it when we return, but back to the point. I thought it would be cousinly to pay my respects to the widow."

"Do you know if there is one?" Potters asked sarcastically, as he delved into a kidney pie.

"One what?"

"A widow."

"There's always a widow, or a son, or a daughter at least. I thought you'd be pleased at my taking such an interest," the viscount teased lightly.

"This is not what I had in mind, not at all," Potters told him scathingly.

"It will do for a start. Think of the character it will give me."

"Character, bah! You are simply bored with London and wish a drive in the country," his lordship noted. "But I will send a note to Mother. Must protect the innocent inhabitants of the country, you know," he ended, "especially the widow."

"Bartone was ninety if he was a day," hooted the viscount derisively. "His widow is as safe from me as if she were already in her tomb," he stated adamantly, failing to recall that words spoken in haste are oft the ones which return to haunt.

CHAPTER FOUR

The excitement of her first journey dulled Mathilda's senses to many of the discomforts of the mailcoach. The brilliant green countryside swept past her eyes with amazing speed as she tried to take it all in. Queen's slipper and false daisy dotted the lush green in masses of white and yellow. Mathilda feasted on this panorama and did not notice the overly earthy odors of her fellow passengers nor the coarse language which spewed from the seats above at every rut and curve.

Sir Bartone had told her of the mailcoaches—how they were steadily increasing their speed, lessening travel time throughout the kingdom—and of the new experimental roads, which she wished there were more of as they hit a particularly rough section of road. Finding herself in the midst of these new experiences, her spirit soared as it had never done before. Even the innkeeper's wife at Darking, with her disapproving glare for the lone young woman, had not daunted her. She was on an adventure and meant to enjoy every minute. By the time the coach halted at Farnham, however, enough of the thrill had worn away for Mathilda to acknowledge a tinge of soreness and some stiffness as she climbed from the coach. It was near noon when they arrived, and the passengers hurried toward the Cat and Mouse to eat. Fingering her reticule, Mathilda decided first to try to locate Squire Pellum's residence. Surely refreshments would be offered to a weary traveler there, she thought. Questioning the first man who came out of the Cat and Mouse, she learned only that he too was a stranger here, but a passing farm lad, about to make his way home after delivering vegetables to the inn, overheard her question.

"Pardon, mum—lady," he said, pulling uneasily at his forelock, "but I pass by Squire's Pellum's."

"Then you can tell me how far it is. Can I walk there?" Mathilda asked eagerly.

"No, mum. I'd say you wouldn't want to be walkin' that far. 'Tis several furlongs from here. 'Haps you can hire a gig from the stables here." He pointed to the massive coaching stables with which the inn served the mailcoaches as well as private travelers. The yard bustled with post chaises and coaches of all sorts.

Fingering her coins once more, Mathilda eyed the farm cart and the sturdy-looking pony of the lad. "Could you not take me to the squire's?" she asked.

"Milady," he said, taken aback, "all I have is this old cart—not fit for the likes o' you."

"If it is no matter to me what I ride in, it should not trouble you. Since you know where the squire lives, you can stop while we are still out of sight of his home and they need never know how I came," she said firmly, walking to the rear of the cart.

Second thoughts arose as she saw the state of the cart's floor, but the youth eagerly flung down his outer frock for her to sit on. Assuring herself it was best to save a shilling or two than to spend them, she told him to fetch her luggage. When he returned, she was seated upon the frock and instructed the portmanteau to be placed next to her. Once out of sight of the town, Mathilda relaxed and marveled at the hedged country lanes which had, fortunately, recently been dragged and smoothed. The floor of the cart was becoming harder with every jounce, and Mathilda hated to reflect what the ride would have been if the winter's ruts and quagmires had not been tended. She learned from the talkative youth that the squire had four daughters and a son and that, while he was well thought of, his wife was feared for her temper.

"We be there, milady," the lad said as he halted his pony at a crossroads. "I must turn here. The squire's house be behind that stone wall ahead. There is a gate in the wall. Will you be wantin' your bag carried?"

"No, I can manage it well enough. Here, take this for your trouble," she said, holding out some coins, which the boy refused. Bidding him farewell, Mathilda picked up her portmanteau with a firm grip, clutched closely the small chest she had held all the way from Horley, and began the march to the squire's. The rumbling of her stomach as she passed through the gate and the dryness of her throat made her rush the last few steps. In her hurry she saw the Tudor manor, with its daub and wattle upper story, as a welcome sight. Hoping no one would hear the hungry rumblings of her stomach, she knocked upon the door.

It swung open almost immediately, and a thin, young maid, her face almost hidden by a huge mobcap, peered out at Mathilda. "What is it ye be wantin', mum?" she asked shyly.

"Nellie, who is it?" a second, firmer voice asked before Mathilda could answer. A young woman of her own age advanced to the door and gave her a cool, scrutinizing stare.

"My name is Mathilda Bartone. My husband was Sir Howard," she began nervously.

"Uncle Howard was unmarried," the young woman said coldly, and reached to close the door.

"But he was," protested Mathilda, stepping into the opening. "He wrote to Mrs. Pellum at the time we were wed and I wrote also to tell of his illness."

Distrusting eyes glared with unbelief.

"Here," Mathilda said, thrusting the small wooden chest forward. "Take this to Mrs. Pellum. She will recognize it or at least the items in it— mementos of her childhood at Bartone Hollows."

The woman's glare wavered as she eyed the chest. Her mother, Mrs. Pellum, had spoken of such an item, but the young woman bearing it did not seem a likely wife for old Uncle Howard. Why, her mother had said he was wealthy, and this woman was dressed in cloth of common quality. Her eyes took in the chest and caused her to falter. Uncle Howard had been wealthy, a fact that had been grilled into the Pellum daughters as their mother oft bemoaned the fact that her brother was too miserly to share. "Mother is out on a morning call with my sisters. Could you not return this eve?"

Dismay crossed Mathilda's features. Hunger, thirst, and exhaustion had taken their toll. "But . . . my coach has already left. It is much too far for me to walk. Could I not await her return here?" she asked.

Indecision flared upon the other; to her own surprise, Mathilda sought to use it, saying, "I know it will be all right. Mrs. Pellum will be most pleased to have the chest. Where shall I await her?" She walked further into the house and set down her portmanteau.

"About your work, Nellie," Miss Pellum scolded

the gawking young maid. "This way," she said coldly to Mathilda.

Following with a relieved smile, Mathilda wondered at the coldness of her reception, then eased her discomfort with the thought that Sir Bartone must have instructed Mrs. Pellum to tell no one about the doll. With her thoughts turned toward the object of her journey, she casually commented as she glanced about the low-ceilinged parlour the young woman had taken her to, "At Bartone Hollows Sir Bartone has a family portrait. Of course, he pointed out each of his family. Your mother was quite a pretty child. I was disappointed to see that the doll she held in the painting was not in this chest, for it is . . ."

"Doll in Red," laughed Miss Pellum harshly. "My pardon for interrupting," she added. "It is that our mother has spoken oft of the doll, and it seems odd that you should mention it. It was her favourite, and she oft told us how her sister, Lady Pennypiece, took it to London with her."

"The doll was taken to London?" Mathilda asked with a sinking heart.

"Years and years ago I imagine—before mother was married. It must have meant quite a lot to her," snapped the young woman, thinking of her mother's grumblings over it. "You had best be seated while I return to my duties." The sound of the outer door opening, and voices entering the house, caused her to raise her hand to her lips.

"Oh, I hope I have not done wrong," she breathed.

A tall, thinner, colder copy of the young woman strode into the parlour. "What is this nonsense about Howard's wife being here?" she demanded loudly.

"I am Lady Bartone," Mathilda answered weakly.

"There is no Lady Bartone—only a strumpet who dares to lay claim to the family's fortune," was blasted at her.

"I have brought this to you from Bartone Hollows," Mathilda said, hoping her voice was steadier than her quivering legs.

Snatching the chest, Mrs. Pellum pointed to the door. "Out of my house. Out!" she shouted, taking a step toward Mathilda, who bolted for the door. "And know that we have a solicitor who will see that you don't get a single shilling," followed her as she grabbed her portmanteau, still sitting just inside the outer door, and staggered for the lane. When the hedge concealed her from view of the house, she halted and sat upon her bag, trying to regain her breath. Her first thought was to burst into tears, but she stayed the impulse as anger overcame any trepidation she had felt.

"How dare that woman," she said aloud, standing. "I shall go back this instant and tell her . . ." Tell her what? She finished the thought silently and sagged back upon the portmanteau as she realized the futility of confronting Mrs. Pellum.

Glancing up and down the lane with a huge sigh, she began to realize her predicament. She had neither eaten nor drunk since early morn and the distance to Farnham was much too far for her to reach by nightfall. "I can only hope someone with a kind heart comes along," she said aloud, stoutly, as she stood once more. Picking up her portmanteau, she began plodding forward, wondering why she had allowed Mrs. Bertie to pack so much into the steadily weightier bag.

An hour later, Mathilda halted for the sixth time. Finding her kerchief, she dabbed at her cheeks and forehead. The pleasant English countryside had become miserably warm and frighteningly solitary.

"Whatever am I to do?" she asked herself, raising her eyes to the cloudless sky.

In answer came the sound of hooves and the rattle of a carriage. Grabbing her portmanteau, Mathilda dashed from the center of the lane as a team and gig dashed by in a cloud of dust. Fanning and coughing as the haze cleared, she saw the vehicle had been pulled to a stop, and the driver was motioning her to come forward.

Anger washed away her tiredness as she stamped forward. "That was entirely uncalled for. Do you always drive with such unconcern?" she demanded.

"I always try to avoid running down young ladies, especially pretty ones," a suave voice returned. "My apologies," he continued, doffing his
hat with his free hand. "How is it you came to be
alone in an English lane? You are not of this area,
for I know all the beautiful women here," the tall
man noted, winking in a most ungentlemanly way.

Blushing, Mathilda stepped back, her anger de-
serting her. "I . . . I am Lady Bartone. Through
some misunderstanding my coach has not come,"
she offered weakly.

"So I see," noted the stranger, with a kindly
smile. "I am at your service, my lady," he offered,
holding out his free hand to assist her into the gig.
"My name is Kittridge." He gave a gallant bow.

"I hardly think I should . . ." began Mathilda.
"We have not been . . ."

"Darkness will have fallen long before you can
walk to Farnham. Few could fault your accepting
assistance," Kittridge coaxed.

A long glance at the lane ahead caused Mathilda
to sigh. Turning her sight to the brightly painted
gig and cushioned seat, she studied the tall gentleman. He was flawlessly dressed in breeches and
frock coat, his hat barely concealing the smooth
blondness of his hair.

"I can do you little harm. I shall give my word
to keep both hands upon the reins," he told her
with perfect innocence. The matched cinnamon
geldings tossed their heads as if to agree.

"I suppose there is no other choice," Mathilda admitted.

"I am sorry to be of so little assistance," he said with an apologetic grimace as he took the portmanteau she handed him. "But I dare not let them go. It has been too long since I had them out."

"They are a beautifully matched pair," Mathilda said as she maneuvered herself into the seat beside him. Safely seated, she straightened her skirts and reached to adjust her bonnet.

Kittridge chose this moment to relax his hold on the team and they sprang forward, throwing Mathilda awkwardly toward the outside of the gig. In her fright, she grabbed hold of the first thing available, and pulled herself aright. Only as Kittridge slowed the team's pace did she realize it was the skirt of his coat that she clung to. Releasing her hold, she saw with dismay that she had bunched and wrinkled the coat-skirt. Awkwardly, she reached to try to smooth it.

Kittridge glanced down at her touch. The large, hazel eyes, surrounded by worry wrinkles, and the contritely pouted lips struck a strange note within him.

Seeing that he watched her, Mathilda blushed and stammered an apology. "I . . . I did not . . . mean to . . ."

"There is little harm done—a hot iron will correct it," he answered kindly. "It was my doing in not controlling these high-steppers. I hope you were not too badly frightened."

"No, in fact, I found it . . . exciting." She regretted her words immediately, as Kittridge laughed.

"Now you are offended—forgive me," he urged her smoothly. "You said you are Lady Bartone?" he asked, pursuing another line to put her at ease. "Are you then related to Squire Pellum's wife?"

"I am . . . was her sister-in-law. My husband, her brother, passed away a short time ago," Mathilda said, studying her black-gloved hands intently.

Resisting the question her reply brought to mind in light of Mrs. Pellum's age, Kittridge gazed curiously at Mathilda's bowed head and launched into a discussion of the countryside, which soon brought her to good spirits, just as he had hoped.

For Mathilda the miles passed as quickly as minutes, as she enjoyed Kittridge's engaging conversation. Much too soon, they entered the bustling stable yard of the Cat and Mouse. A stable boy dashed to Kittridge's team's heads and held them. Kittridge jumped down lightly and handed Mathilda down.

"I thank you for your kindness," she told him as he reached for her portmanteau.

"Will you stay the night?" he asked.

"No, arrangements have been made for my passage on the mailcoach. I should be in time for the last departure that will take me on my way to Horley, but . . ." Mathilda paused as she realized she would have to inquire if this was true.

"Let us go to the inn and get some refreshment, and I will check for you. If necessary, I will arrange rooms for you," he told her.

"Oh, that is most kind of you, for I must admit I have not traveled much," Mathilda said with relief. She gladly took the arm he offered.

Some time later, the arrangements settled, they waited for the mailcoach to arrive.

"I am most grateful," Mathilda told Kittridge. "This would have been rather more than I could manage. It was very kind of you to help me."

"A most enjoyable experience, I assure you," he told her, smiling.

The sound of a horn in the distance turned both their heads. "There is the coach now," he said regretfully.

Neither spoke as it came into view and finally drew to a halt a short distance from them. Amid the clamour of changing teams and passengers, the two stood unmoving.

"I suppose I must go," Mathilda said. "Thank you once again."

Kittridge followed and handed her into the coach. "Safe journey" was all he said in farewell.

The coach lurched into movement almost immediately and Mathilda fought down the urge to wave at Kittridge, who still stood watching. He tipped his hat just as the coach turned onto the main road, leaving the inn and all those about it behind.

Taking assessment as she adjusted to the coach's jumping, rocking movements, Mathilda decided she had fared well. She certainly had had a surfeit of excitement. How fortunate Mr. Kittridge had appeared, she thought with a smile. Such a kind gentleman. She sighed, placing the memory gently away in her mind. Doll in Red had not been found and her future had no place for daydreams such as Mr. Kittridge inspired.

CHAPTER FIVE

"Rather neglected, wouldn't you say?" Potters quipped as the viscount drew the landau to a halt before Bartone Hollows. "I thought you said the old boy was in funds."

"So I was told," Bartone said, viewing the two-story stone house with distaste, for it stood alone amidst a sea of winter-old weeds and the paint about the windows and doors was peeling.

"Someone was incorrect."

"Evidently. Perhaps it would be best not to make our presence known," the viscount muttered, taking in the ragged untrimmed trees and overgrown flowerbeds.

"Too late, old man. Butler, I'd say," Potters said, tapping Bartone on the arm. "This was your idea," he smirked.

Dannon ran his eyes over the landau, which was fashionably painted in red and yellow. The two men he judged to be of the "quality," their bearing as well as their clothing and equipage indicating as much. "My lords," he bowed.

As he spoke, Old Jerry managed to get to the heads of the viscount's teams. A twitch of Bartone's eyebrow suggested that he doubted the man's ability to hold them safely, but he stepped down lightly. "I wish to see Lady Bartone," he commanded.

"Madame is not at home," Dannon answered coldly.

"Then I shall await her return. See my teams are taken care of and show my friend and me to a pleasant room," the viscount ordered crisply.

Recognizing a voice accustomed to obedience, Dannon hesitated to cut the man as he wished. Obviously the gentleman felt himself to be of some importance. "Madame is away from home, visiting family in Farnham. However, I think she would not wish anyone turned away."

"In Farnham, you say? Deuced unfortunate. I have come from London to extend my condolences at the loss of Sir Bartone. But at least a glass of brandy before we go on. Better make that tea for Potters, here," Bartone ordered, walking up the steps and through the doors.

Lord Potters grimaced and followed.

Expressionlessly, Dannon came after them, his annoyance and dislike for the young buck's arrogance growing. "In here, my lords," he said, opening the door to the small parlour. "I shall bring your refreshments."

"Very good—be quick about it. I don't mean to dawdle here all day," Bartone said impatiently.

At the end of the corridor, Dannon encountered Mrs. Bertie. "Who is that acting like this is his house? What does he mean raising his voice to you? I'll tell him where to dawdle."

"Calm yourself and make the tea," Dannon whispered. "Wait until I learn who they are."

Muttering to herself, Mrs. Bertie plodded away to the kitchen while Dannon headed for the wine cellar.

"Where is that man?" the viscount asked irritably as he sat staring at Potters.

"You did ask for tea," his friend said defensively. "I rather imagine they had to make a fire to warm the water, with Lady Bartone not being here."

Rising, Bartone strode about the small room while Potters remained relaxed upon the sofa. "Sit down—it will come soon. I don't imagine he wants us here any longer than necessary from the look he threw you. What are we to do now?"

"We shall make for London. I'll not stay here. We should be able to make it by morn."

"You mean to go all night? Impossible!"

"Only to you, Potts. You can stay at the first inn we pass if you wish. I have seen all I need here."

He halted to inspect a portrait above the fireplace. "This must be Bartone. Done by Reynolds, no less," he noted with approving surprise.

"My lords," Dannon announced, as he entered with the tea and brandy.

Bartone sat down as Dannon set the tray upon a side table. "You may serve us," he commanded unnecessarily.

Dannon's opinion of the young man's brashness did not show as he pointedly poured the tea, serving the companion first.

"How long will Lady Bartone be away?" the viscount asked as he took the glass of brandy Dannon offered on the tray.

"I could not say, my lord."

"Is her ladyship in good health?" Potters asked, trying to lighten his friend's highhandedness.

"Yes, my lord. Who shall I say has inquired?" Dannon asked, making good use of the opening.

Pulling one of his cards from his inner coat, the viscount tossed it upon the tray. "Tell Lady Bartone that I am sorry to have missed her." He quaffed the brandy down and returned the glass to the tray. "Come, Potts," he called, striding towards the door.

"Thank Lady Bartone for her hospitality," Potters told Dannon and followed after the hurrying figure. "That was rather harsh of you," he scolded as he climbed up beside Bartone.

"Harsh?" shrugged the other. "Who is to say?

Servants need to be kept in their place. Besides, who can know—Bartone Hollows may fall to me upon the widow's death. Could be mine already." He laid the whip to the teams, preventing any words Potters had in mind to say.

"What is wrong, Dannon?" Mrs. Bertie asked, seeing the stricken look upon her husband's face when he brought the tea tray back to the kitchen. "Are you ill?" She stepped forward anxiously.

"No. It is he."

"What are you saying? Did one of those dandies harm you?" she questioned, puzzled by his words.

"The young lords—one was the viscount." Doom filled his voice.

"Viscount?" she paused. "Viscount Bartone," Mrs. Bertie breathed, as the implication of his particular presence came to mind. She sagged into a chair. "Do you think he knows?" she asked weakly.

"He acted as if he were lord of the house," Dannon answered.

"But don't all young bucks act a bit that way?" she asked hopefully.

"I suppose," Dannon replied, thinking carefully as he set the tray down and removed the dishes. "But his coming here as soon after sir's death . . . especially after he has never shown any interest in his cousin before. No, there has to be a reason for it. He must know or suspect something."

Raising her apron to cover her face, Mrs. Bertie began to cry.

"Now, now, dear. Don't fret so. Madame has ten months left. Why, she may have the doll now," Dannon told her awkwardly, patting his wife's shoulder. "You'll see," he told her firmly. "Sir Bartone did not mean that young coxcomb to have Bartone Hollows."

CHAPTER SIX

Lacking Dannon's confidence, Old Jerry did not ask, only guessed at the fate of his mistress's journey as he drove the gig toward Bartone Hollows after meeting the mailcoach. The droop of her shoulders, the worrying frown, and her failure to ask about his arthritis were ominous signs of failure.

"Good day, madam." Dannon greeted Mathilda as she tiredly mounted the steps. His reserved expression became colder, somewhat constrained, as he watched her abject approach. Taking her light travel cloak and gloves, he said, "Tea will be brought to the library, madam. May we speak with you then?"

Mathilda nodded and slowly trudged forward. Pressing tears were stayed by the mental grit garnered through childhood years of poverty. Dutiful inclination had overcome whatever thoughts she had given to not returning to the Hollows; she would see this to the end.

Dannon solemnly served the hot tea and dainty biscuits and discreetly withdrew. But Mathilda knew in only a few moments the three would come. Safe once more in her own home, she slowly relaxed as the tea warmed her.

The comfort of the excellent tea was robbed by the entrance of the eager smile of Mrs. Bertie. Mathilda's cup clanked loudly into the saucer as she finished the tea abruptly. For a time, only the ticking of the large clock at the end of the library sounded. To Mathilda, the deep, steady tone said, "doom . . . doom." Words did not come easily as she studied the shoes of the respectfully waiting trio.

The lines of Mrs. Bertie's smile weakened and collapsed completely when Mathilda raised her eyes to meet theirs.

"As you can see," Mathilda began, "I have returned in failure."

"Did you question Mrs. Pellum most closely as to where the doll may be?" Dannon asked quietly.

"Well . . . no," Mathilda answered, hesitant to tell them of her treatment at the hands of that lady. "But I did speak with a daughter about it," she added quickly as she saw their sagging expressions.

"What did she say, miss?" Mrs. Bertie asked, stepping closer.

"She said that the doll had been taken by Mrs.

Pellum's sister many years past when she moved to London," Mathilda replied abjectly.

"London," breathed Dannon. "London," he spoke a second time with conviction. Why, it makes sense, he said to himself, then addressed his mistress. "Madam, when shall you depart?"

Confusion flared on Mathilda's upraised face.

Mrs. Bertie clapped her hands. "Right you are, Dannon," she bubbled. "London it is. But you, miss, you need a day's rest, and then there is your wardrobe to consider. There's likely not much in it that is fashionable for London, but if we both work—for your stitching is most accomplished—I believe we could be ready in a sennight."

Awareness dawning, Mathilda shook her head vigourously. "No," burst from her as she rose. "I shall not. I cannot," she objected, wringing her hands.

"Why, miss, what can you mean?" asked Mrs. Bertie, putting an arm comfortingly about Mathilda's shoulders. "Of course you can."

Lady Bartone threw a stricken glance at Dannon. Surely his common sense would put an end to this.

"Did something untoward occur when you were at Squire Pellum's?" he asked. "In truth, we had not looked for your return this soon. It is as if you arrived and began your return journey on the same day."

His words brought to mind a question that had been on her lips when she stepped from the mail-coach to see Old Jerry awaiting her. It had been forgotten as her mind was taken with how to explain her failure without giving too many details. "How did you know I was returning this day? I had wondered what I must do, and was so thankful to see you there," she smiled warmly at Old Jerry. "Surely you were not meeting every coach?"

"A messenger arrived only yesterday with a note advising us of the time and day of your return," Dannon answered.

"A messenger? But I sent none."

"I thought it odd you would, and the note was not in your hand—a most masculine script. Perhaps you mentioned the need to notify us to a fellow traveler?"

"No, I spoke to no one, as Mrs. Bertie advised. Was there no signature?"

"Only the monogram K, madam."

K, thought Mathilda, then recognition came. Mr. Kittridge. A warm smile came to her lips.

"Then you did speak with someone?" Mrs. Bertie asked, noting her look.

"Yes. A most proper gentleman, who rescued me from . . ." She stopped abruptly, alarmed at her slip.

"Rescued you, madam?" Dannon inquired. "Then something is amiss. Since your journey indirectly involves us all, I daresay we should know the particulars," he prompted gently.

She thought to fabricate something minor, but the set of their faces told her only the truth would suffice. The truth, she thought, will end this nonsense about London. They must see if I cannot handle a squire's wife, I certainly would be no match for a lady in London. Even this thought did not make the telling easy, for Mathilda knew the pride in which Dannon held the Bartone name. "A Mr. Kittridge was kind enough to take me to Farnham from Squire Pellum's," she began at last.

"Ah, a friend they introduced you to," Mrs. Bertie noted, nodding approvingly.

"Not quite." Mathilda plunged forward with the tale. "He stopped his gig after passing me in the lane not far from the squire's house."

"In the lane? Were you walking? Unescorted?" Mrs. Bertie asked indignantly.

"Mrs. Pellum would not receive you?" Dannon asked tonelessly.

"She was not at home. One of her daughters admitted me—most reluctantly," Mathilda told them. Speaking as cryptically as possible, she told them all, ending with, ". . . so it must be clear to you that we must do with what is left of the bequest. Perhaps Mrs. Pellum has a solicitor already calling upon Mr. Petersbye trying to deprive us of even that."

"They cannot be about that so soon, but now I

see why *he* came," Dannon said, thinking aloud.

"He? Did someone call while I was gone?"

"You should have seen him, miss," Mrs. Bertie began excitedly. "Tall and dark—sinister, weren't he, Dannon?" She looked to her husband for affirmation. "Like those savages we hear spoke of in the colonies. Why, he acted as if the Hollows 'twere his."

Dannon nodded, a frown covering his features. "The Viscount Bartone and a friend called yesterday. He demanded refreshments, and his manner was most . . . disrespectful. I fear he must know of the will's stipulation."

"Then there is naught for us to do," Mathilda said hopelessly.

"I will not believe that," Dannon replied. "But we must act quickly. You must go to London as soon as possible and call upon Sir Bartone's other sister—Lady Pennypiece."

"How dare I? My reception will be the same as Mrs. Pellum gave me. It would be a futile waste of our funds."

"That may be true," Mrs. Bertie said, looking to her husband for guidance.

"I do not believe Lady Pennypiece will be of the same mind as Mrs. Pellum," Dannon said sternly, defending his idea. "There is no question but that you must go to her at once and tell her all." Surveying the unconvinced women, he continued. "It is our only hope. If Mrs. Pellum chooses to take action, we may lose all," he lied forcefully, "for there are few here, pardon me, madam, who would not agree with her. The viscount's appearance is an ominous sign that he and she have communicated and are setting a joint course of action. Lady Pennypiece was always of a different mind than her sister in the days when I knew of them. We can only pray age has not altered that. She may well be willing to come to our aid. Madam," he faced Mathilda squarely. "You know what our fate will be if the doll is not found. I can honestly say I believe there is no hope to be placed in the viscount's generosity. For our sakes, you must go."

A tremor went through Mathilda as she looked at the three. A journey to Farnham to see a squire's wife was one thing, but to go to London?

"You are the widow of Sir Bartone, madam," Dannon told her. "As brave and true an Englishman as ever lived. You can take pride in his name and draw strength from what he taught you. I am certain he would wish you to. He would not tolerate the treatment accorded his wife or home by his relations."

Dannon's words prodded a spark of pride, of resentment. *He is right*, she decided. Straightening her shoulders under a new resolve, Mathilda thought, *I owe it to Bartone not to let them do as they will. Why, they did not even have the courtesy to . . . Well, they certainly had no love for*

*him. We received not a word from any of them,
not even when he died.* Her ire rose higher. *But
now they want to divide what is his to give. Bartone would have put them in their place. I will do
it.*

Spurred on by the feeling of the moment, she
announced, "I will depart for London in the morn.
Mrs. Bertie, you can send my belongings later. I
doubt that I shall require much. I can let you
know after I see the lay of things. They shall see
that Sir Bartone's widow will not be ignored."

Brave words, she chided herself—*may they last
all the way to London.*

CHAPTER SEVEN

The hackney driver accepted the coins Mathilda gave him with a resigned grimace. These country folk, he thought as he drove on, are always tight with their purse.

Behind him Mathilda surveyed the houses about Golden Square. No longer filled with the finest of the aristocracy, it still was regarded as a reputable neighborhood. Facing Lady Penny-piece's door, No. 31, she glanced to the right and left. There was nothing to do but knock. Her hand was reaching for the large brass knocker when the door swung open, startling her.

"What is your business, miss?" a sonorous voice asked.

Being of average height, Mathilda found herself peering at the butler's stomach. Slowly her eyes traveled upward, past the golden braids adorning his red-gold livery jacket, past the epaulets on the broad, full shoulders, and on to a craggy face, which was frowning fiercely. "Your business?" the huge man repeated.

"I . . . wish to speak with Lady Pennypiece," Mathilda managed, unable to take her eyes from the massive gloved hand that still held the door. "On a matter of personal interest."

"Who be you?" the giant demanded.

"Lady Bartone," she said, gulping.

Dipping his head in what Mathilda took for a bow, he beckoned her to enter. "Sit there." A huge finger pointed to a chair close by the door.

Mathilda took her seat quickly and watched the towering form stalk away. She was amazed the walls and floor did not shake with the weight of his tread.

While she waited, she studied the various items in the small hall. Brass sconces were highly polished; the oak paneling was waxed and shined to a reflecting degree. One piece drew her attention above all others—the longcase clock. Its oak cabinet with marquetry panels of gilded bouquets of fall flowers was beautiful to behold.

Heavy footsteps brought her present purpose back to mind.

"This way, miss," the butler called from the end of the hall.

Suppressing a smile at the thought of what Dannon's opinion of this rough-mannered giant would be, Mathilda rose and carefully smoothed the skirts of her black silk. She followed him up the stairs, then down a narrow corridor and up a second flight, which led to an airy, wide corridor.

"Through the doors," the butler ordered, pointing toward double French doors that stood open at the end of the hall.

Seeing nothing in the room but open space and undraped windows on the far wall, Mathilda hesitated.

"Her ladyship can't waste all day waitin' for ye," menaced the huge man behind her.

"Of course not," Mathilda answered, stepping toward the doors hurriedly. She glanced· back as she reached the doors and found he was still watching her. With no escape possible, she turned to face the room and entered determinedly.

"Ah, a widow in black calls, my lady. But is she a widow?" a high-pitched male voice asked mockingly.

Mathilda twirled to face the speaker and became even more indignant as she saw that the thin, reedy character was staring at her through a quizzing glass.

"Enough," a clear, sharp voice commanded. "Come forward," it ordered Mathilda. "My man says you are Lady Bartone—if so, why the widow's weeds? The viscount was in good health when I saw him at the opera two eves past."

Stepping toward the pair slowly, Mathilda studied the old woman who was seated in the lone chair in the large, empty room. The voice bespoke strength and vigour, but the form showed advanced age. Withered skin on the shrunken form, which sat ramrod straight, told her Lady Pennypiece was near Sir Bartone's age. Her gown was of a style worn twenty years past, and a huge powdered wig was perched atop the aged head. She should be a figure for ridicule, Mathilda thought, but something about her squashed the thought—her bearing perhaps, or the way the eyes bore in and held one. They were stark blue, as brilliant as an October sky, and they pierced Mathilda to the core.

"Speak, child—I am Lady Pennypiece." The old woman spoke more kindly seeing Mathilda's ill-concealed fear.

"I am not Viscount Bartone's wife. My husband was your brother—Sir Howard."

"What? See, she dares to espouse it just as I said. She is young enough to have been Uncle's granddaughter," piped the young man at her ladyship's side.

"Many a man has married a woman much younger than he," returned Mathilda sharply, determined not to relive the embarrassment caused by Mrs. Pellum. "Just as many a young man marries an older woman for her money."

Lady Pennypiece cackled merrily at this, and Mathilda blushed profusely at the thought of what she had said.

"My pardons, my lady," she hastened to say,

giving a curtsy. "But if you had answered my correspondence and come to the Hollows when your brother was dying, you would have seen the proof of who I say I am."

"Quick of tongue, eh? Your place as wife has been challenged before? Howard was no fool—why would he marry one so young as you? Despite your words, you have the look of a milk-and-honey miss."

Hesitant to answer so personal a question in the presence of an unknown gentleman, Mathilda threw a glance his way. "Could we not speak alone, my lady? What I have come to speak of is most . . . private."

"I would think it would be," the old woman taunted mildly. "Let me introduce you to my nephew—our nephew, to be more exact—Richard Pellum."

"Surprised to see me, aren't you? Mother was correct about you. See, Aunt Netta, her guilt shows. She is merely a scheming tart," he finished triumphantly, his vulturelike beak bobbing.

Mathilda did not know whether to flee or attack. Any decision was stopped by the old woman's words. "I will judge her guilt or innocence for myself, Richard. You may go."

"But, Aunt," he objected, "surely I have a right to hear . . ."

"In this house I alone have 'rights,'" Lady Pennypiece haughtily cut off.

"Yes, my lady." Pellum bowed his stick frame meekly. With a glare at Mathilda, he withdrew from the room, his gait not unlike that of a mincing skylark.

"Now, miss, your tale."

"I am not a 'miss,' and it is no 'tale' I have come with," Mathilda dared to answer in the seeming hopelessness of her cause.

"I speak to anyone beneath fifty years of age as miss, and I will decide if what you say is tale or not," returned Lady Pennypiece, her eyes sparking.

"What is the use of my speaking when I know you have no interest in me or your brother? May I ask why you did not come to see Bartone when I wrote that he was dying?" Mathilda questioned softly. The answer would be a final indication of her chances with the countess.

Lady Pennypiece's shrewd eyes swept over Mathilda from head to foot. They narrowed as she challenged the other to meet her gaze. Mathilda did not flinch from it.

"You may not," the countess finally answered and rose. "But come with me, and we shall visit, Lady Bartone." A smile eased the grip of time on the old woman's features and Mathilda felt her fear begin to melt.

Five chimes from a clock in another room in the house in No. 31 Golden Square intruded into

Mathilda's mind. "Why, I have been quite carried away speaking of myself for so long," she said. "I must go, for I have made no arrangements. . . . Perhaps you know of a place I might stay?" she asked. Dropping her eyes, she added, "I still have not spoken of my reason for coming to London."

"I have a fair idea of the reason," Lady Pennypiece said lightly. "Of course you shall stay with me while you are in London. I instructed Hollon to place your things in the Queen Anne room when he announced your arrival."

"But you may not wish me to stay when you hear what I wish of you."

"Which is?"

Leaning forward, her face youthfully earnest, Mathilda spoke. "I . . . we wish your aid in locating an object. You see, Bartone put a stipulation in his will. If we . . . if I cannot locate this object within one year, there is to be nothing for Dannon and the others."

"And for yourself?"

"There would be nothing for myself as well."

"And who is this Dannon?"

"Sir Bartone's man—a lifelong retainer—his butler and valet."

"And you wish to see *him* rewarded?" Lady Pennypiece asked curtly, her suspicion apparent.

Seeing it, Mathilda drew back. "Of course," she said rigidly. "And Mrs. Bertie and Old Jerry."

"Who are these?" her ladyship asked, with a

tinge of mockery in her voice. "Are there any others?"

"Perhaps poor simple Sal. But if I should continue on at the Hollows, there would be no problem, for I should certainly have her remain."

"Who are these people?"

"Mrs. Bertie is Dannon's wife—and our housekeeper and cook. Old Jerry is the head of the stables; Sal helps Mrs. Bertie. She has only been there a few years, but the other three have served their entire lives under Bartone and it is not right they be cast off with nothing for their loyal service."

"What is this object you spoke of?"

"It is known as Doll in Red. I have been given a year to find her and turn her over to Mr. Petersbye. If I fail, what remains of five hundred pounds at the end of the year will be all I have to divide among the three, and that will certainly not be enough to see the old ones comfortably set. Don't you see, I do not mind for myself so much, for I have managed before and can again . . ."

"You mean to have nothing for yourself?" the old woman asked.

"If I fail, only a minimal amount," came the crisply honest answer.

"Doll in Red? I do not recall such an object."

"There is a family portrait at the Hollows done when Mrs. Pellum was slightly more than an infant. In it she is holding a doll which I was told is known as Doll in Red. When I called upon Mrs. Pellum, I was told that the doll had been brought to London by you. Miss Pellum, who told me this, indicated her mother was quite upset at losing it. I was hoping you would recall it and perhaps still have it in your possession," Mathilda ended hopefully.

"It would have been a doll dressed in red," Lady Pennypiece murmured. "Would it have had a parasol?"

"Yes." Excitement surged. "And dark brown locks of hair with black lace edging the flounce of her gown and the gay bonnet."

"A widow like you, eh? Oh, do not take offense," she added, seeing Mathilda's hurt look. "I recall the doll but have not seen it for years."

"Can it be here—in the attics perhaps?"

"I shall see they are searched on the morrow, but now we must dine early," Lady Pennypiece said, rising. "Lady Morrow has asked me to her soiree and I cannot stand the food she serves. You shall attend with me."

"But I cannot. I have not been invited."

"There will be no problem," the other replied imperiously.

"But this is my only gown, my lady. I have nothing fit to wear."

Lady Pennypiece raised her quizzing glass, which hung by a gold chain around her neck. "Quite out of style," she quipped. "If you will not mind being seen in my presence, I shall not mind being seen in yours. Besides, Lady Morrow has told me that Viscount Bartone is invited and I think you would find meeting him a most interesting experience. He has paid little attention to the eligibles of this season and seems intent upon dashing his life away on drink and courtesans. However, he might find a widow in black vastly interesting. Come, child, I think you may make the season."

CHAPTER EIGHT

"No, Potts, I don't mean to go. Harriet Wilson's fête will be infinitely more interesting than Lady Morrow's soiree," Viscount Bartone slurred, and finished his glass of port.

Baron Potters looked to Green, who whispered confidentially, "His lordship just returned from White's a short time ago."

"You agreed to go—told me to stop by for you," Potters said, walking to the table where Bartone sat. "You expressed an interest in seeing Lady Pennypiece." He moved the almost empty port bottle out of the viscount's reach. "Isn't it early to be finishing a bottle already?"

"I hold it well," hiccuped the viscount. " 'Tis my fourth if you must know, and none of your business."

Trying another approach, Potters said, "It would not do any harm to stop at the soiree on the way to Harriet's—that is, if you plan to go out at all this eve. It might be best to remain in."

"No." Bartone reared upright and stood weaving back and forth. "Suppose it wouldn't be any harm to see old Pennypiece first—see if she has the bird yet," he laughed, the pitch unnaturally high.

"Of course not," Potters answered, offering a humble prayer that his friend would pass out on the way. "My landau awaits," he added with forced cheerfulness as he watched Green drape the viscount's cape across the broad shoulders and hand him his hat and gloves. He winced as Green had to pick up the hat twice, finally setting it upon Bartone's head himself. Following his weaving friend to the landau, he deliberated what course of action he should take to halt Bartone's rapid deterioration.

The viscount appeared set upon destroying himself. His drinking and womanizing had accelerated after their return from Horley to such a degree that Potters was becoming desperate. Harriet Wilson's set, with which Bartone now spent most of his time, was encouraging this, and nothing Potters said or did had any effect. Sadly, Lord Potters realized that if something did not jolt the viscount soon, he would be lost, as were so many of the aristocracy, never doing a useful deed their entire lives.

A jolt—but what? How?

* * *

"I should not have come, my lady," Mathilda whispered. "Everyone is staring."

"My dear child, if they did not stare I would be a failure. It pleases them to think me eccentric. Even Mr. Brummel approves of me because I am singular—quaint, I believe he said. One must not disappoint. You are here to enjoy yourself. I cannot believe that life with Howard was very lively. He was old before he reached his majority."

"Sir Bartone . . ." Mathilda began defensively.

"Do not object, I did not mean to insult him. Ah, here is Lady Morrow. Now smile, quite sadly—a tear or two, perhaps."

Mathilda had no chance to guess if Lady Pennypiece was joking, as the old lady swept her forward.

"You must meet Lady Bartone, Agatha," her ladyship commanded. "Howard's dear wife, you know." She paused, enjoying Lady Morrow's startled reaction. "Yes," she continued briskly, "the poor dear was set upon pining away, but I knew you would insist I bring her.

"You look lovely this eve, Agatha—a new gown? Ah, I see my nephew. So good of you to invite him. Later, my dear, later." She waved her hand airily at Lady Morrow and drew Mathilda towards Richard Pellum.

Seeing their approach, Pellum blanched.

"Richard, how good to see you." Lady Pennypiece raised her quizzing glass, causing the young man to squirm. "The music has begun. Off with you both, dancing is for the young." She placed Mathilda's hand in Pellum's. "Now at my age there is the cardroom. Whist, you know." With a wave of her hand she was gone.

The two unwilling companions viewed each other suspiciously, their hands disengaging as soon as Lady Pennypiece's back was turned. Mathilda saw that Pellum was much her own age, not older, as she had first thought. This second encounter revealed nothing to alter her original opinion. With his vulture's face, straight shock of brown hair, and extreme thinness he would have mystified even the blindest mother. His clothing, in shades of ever brighter turquoise, drew attention to areas which were best forgotten.

"I suppose I must dance with you," Pellum finally said gracelessly.

"I would rather you did not, Mr. Pellum. I would be quite happy to forgo the honour," Mathilda replied coldly.

The thin figure relaxed. "Thank you," he said with relief. "Mother would have heard, and I'd never have had any peace. But let me escort you to a chair," he offered in gratitude.

Mentally noting that Pellum was not all bad, Mathilda took the arm he offered and walked with him into the main ballroom. Spying an empty chair along the wall, he led her to it, jerked a bow, and fled.

Mathilda felt like laughing as she watched his retreat but was sobered by the thought that he may be feeling as out of place as she in these surroundings. The smart cutaway jackets, tight knee breeches, and silk hose of the men showed him at as much disadvantage as her high-necked, full-skirted black silk showed her against the women's decolleté, high-waisted gowns of sheer organza, muslin, and tissue. Even the quality of her gown's silk could not redeem it.

Two dances later Mathilda still sat alone, her back becoming straighter and her chin higher as she watched the gay men and women move through a stylish country set and then the allemande, which she had only read about. Oft had she heard about such scenes from the gentry's daughters who were favoured with a "season." All the glamour and beauty they had described seemed even more vivid in reality, intensified by her years of poverty, which the few years of faded glory at Bartone Hollows had not erased. She felt like an intruder, the unwelcome guest, and her eyes kept flitting to the open doors at the far end of the ballroom.

If only I dared rise and escape, she thought. Her moment came as the orchestra signaled a pause and everyone milled about the dance floor. Mathilda rose and edged her way between the various clusters of gentlemen and ladies. Heaving a sigh of relief, she escaped onto the terrace. Couples walked the paths of the small garden just off it, seeing no one but themselves. Not wishing to draw attention to herself, she walked into the shadows offered by a pair of yews at one side of the terrace.

A full moon brightened the dark May night with a soft sheen of light. Large planters of pansies and tubs of tulips were set around the sculptured shrubbery of the garden and at the edges of the terrace. The flowers reminded Mathilda of the few scraggly tulips that struggled into bloom each spring in the badly tended gardens of Bartone Hollows; melancholy settled upon her.

Indoors the music struck up once more, and the couples in the garden hurried into the ballroom. A loud burst of drunken laughter and the crash of a tray of glasses drew a frown to Mathilda's face. She came from the shadows and sat upon the balustrade. Wishing to forget where she was, she drank in the beauty of the delicate pansy blossoms and the stately standing tulips, then raised her face to the golden moon. The mellow light played softly against the black silk of her gown, giving it a shimmering glow which was reflected in her features, upon which weighed a deep sadness. She thought of all the dreams she had never dared to enjoy, even as a young girl. Now, among the soft scent of the flowers with the flowing strains of music in the air and the moon smiling down upon her, she thought of Kittridge and happiness flared briefly, followed by deeper melancholy.

To Potters's dismay the fresh night air revived the viscount. He hoped the stay at Lady Morrow's would be brief enough to prevent Bartone from adding another incident to his reputation. This hope deserted him as his friend staggered against a footman, sending a tray of drink-filled glasses crashing to the floor in the ballroom.

"Get some air on the terrace while I make apologies," Lord Potters whispered harshly to his friend.

Suprisingly, the viscount did as he was bid, and came onto the terrace just when Mathilda sat. His bemused mind was drawn by the solitary figure, so stark in black against the moonlight and so sorrowful. As he gazed upon her, he felt his mind clear, and a desire to smooth the sadness from her face swept over him. Quietly, soberly, Bartone stepped toward Mathilda, halting a step from her.

His presence turned Mathilda's head. Her eyes left the sweet, consoling moon and met Bartone's hungry gaze. Place, time, and circumstance were all forgotten. All of Mathilda's suppressed longings flared in answer to the naked yearning and searching wonder in Bartone's features.

He reached out and brushed her cheek. "You are not a spirit," he breathed. "Your skin has the glow of pearls, your eyes the glitter of diamonds—but you could never be cold and hard." His hand took hers; he drew her up.

Mesmerized by each other, the pair stood entranced.

"Will! Will, where have you gone to?" a voice intruded.

Mathilda drew a sharp breath and pulled her hand from the viscount's, but her eyes could not leave his. Neither did she move away as the viscount leaned slowly forward. Their lips met softly in a tender caress.

"Will," Potters called as he came onto the terrace, "are you here?"

His words broke the spell, returning Mathilda to the present, making her aware of the strong odor of drink about the man before her. With a gasp, she drew back. Alarm, embarrassment flared. Giving Bartone a wild look, she fled past him, past Potters, and into the ballroom.

"What have you done now?" Potters asked the viscount accusingly. "Can I not leave you alone for a moment?" He took in the strange look upon Bartone's face. "Is something wrong? Are you all right?"

"You saw her? Is she real?" Bartone asked in a shaking voice.

"I have never known you to kiss spirits—not your type, I'd say," Potters laughed nervously. "Come, old boy, I think it time I took you home.

You've had too much to drink if a simple kiss upsets you."

"I must find her," Bartone said, stumbling forward.

"Don't think that would be wise in your state, Will. Let me take you home," Lord Potters urged.

"No, I must know who she is," the viscount slurred and lurched from Potters's hold, going toward the doors.

Inside, Mathilda had collided full force with a gentleman, spilling his drink over both of them. Completely flustered and in a panic, she tried unsuccessfully to stammer an apology.

The man was making light of it when suddenly he took hold of her arm. "Lady Bartone," he exclaimed, "what a pleasant encounter!"

At the sound of her name, Mathilda forced her eyes to focus upon the man. "Mr. Kittridge. Thank heavens. Oh, I am so sorry." She brushed at his jacket.

"It is nothing—certainly a minor inconvenience if it reveals your presence. Where were you going in such a rush?" he laughed.

Glancing back toward the doors, then to Kittridge, she said urgently, "Do you know where the cardroom is? Can you take me there?" Another backward glance revealed Bartone, striding haphazardly toward her.

Kittridge followed her gaze and saw her panic. Tapping a passing footman, he ordered, "Take

Lady Bartone to the cardroom." To Mathilda he said, "Go, I will take care of this matter." With a warm smile he urged her to go. She followed the footman eagerly.

At Bartone's approach, Kittridge blocked his path. "I think you had better leave, Bartone."

"You've nothing to do with this," the viscount snapped.

"The lady wants nothing to do with you. I will not have you forcing your attentions upon her, family claim or no," Kittridge stated calmly.

"Come, Will, let us leave," Potters urged, having caught up with his friend.

"Go with Baron Potters, Bartone. When you have recovered your sensibilities, you can apologize to Lady Bartone."

Befuddled, the viscount turned to Potters. "When did I wed?" he asked, bewildered, then shook himself and confronted Kittridge.

"You can call upon her tomorrow," he said quietly.

The clear, sober tones of the other had a calming effect upon Bartone. Drink had put his thoughts in total confusion, and he did not object as Kittridge and Potters led him out of the ballroom.

Sinking into the landau's seat, Bartone mumbled, "He called her Bartone. Why, Potts? Lady Bartone?" He murmured her name once more as he dozed off to sleep.

Lord Potters heaved a sigh of relief and ordered his driver to Bartone's residence. He was not certain what had happened on the terrace, but it was evident that the viscount had been given a jolt. Now, Lord Potters thought, will the effect be good or harmful? Will he be rescued from his ways, or plunged to their depths? And what part did Kittridge play in this? "Lady Bartone," he said aloud. "How interesting." He settled back with a smile.

CHAPTER NINE

The worst of her panic had subsided by the time Mathilda reached the cardroom. Embarrassment and confusion came in its stead. Looking over the players, she was amazed to see so many women. Countess Pennypiece's wig made locating her no problem, but Mathilda decided not to interrupt her, seeing the intensity with which she was playing.

"You wish to be seated, madam?" a liveried servant asked.

"No, no, I was just leaving," Mathilda said, and retreated to the corridor, only to find herself at more of a loss there. To avoid the disdainful looks of the fashionably dressed women, she devoted her full attention to the portraits and paintings hung along the corridor. The scenes and faces did not register as she searched vainly for an escape. Each second was an hour of mortification.

"Lady Bartone, I had hoped you would not leave," Kittridge said, halting at her side. "Let us get some refreshmnt. The viscount has departed and will not trouble you further," he added, seeing Mathilda look warily past his shoulder.

A viscount, she thought. *Whatever possessed me to let him kiss me? A man I didn't even know.*

"You are not pleased to see me?" asked Kittridge at her frowning response to his suggestion.

"It is not you—I could not be happier to renew your acquaintance. It seems my debt of gratitude to you is ever increased," she smiled.

"My honour, I assure you." He offered his arm, which Mathilda accepted. "I did not know you planned to come to London. Will you be staying long?" he asked as they walked down the corridor.

"No. Well, I am uncertain. There are some matters I must see to, and I am unsure of the length of time it will take. I must leave as soon as the answer is known."

"Then I must hope you are not successful," Kittridge said, halting to gaze at her.

His words brought suspicion to her features.

"Immediately, that is. What have I said to deserve such a scowl?" he asked as they walked on.

"Nothing. It is nothing. I was just thinking of . . ."

"Not still dwelling on Bartone, are you? He is a sad case. It seemed likely he would be a real asset when he first returned from the West Indies. We had high hopes he would assume his seat in the Lords and work for the betterment of the country, but he seems intent on wasting his talents. His reputation for womanizing and drinking grows even larger. I am sorry he has upset you."

This time Mathilda halted. "You mean the man who . . . who was following me was . . . is Viscount Bartone?" she asked in disbelief.

"Why, yes. I took for granted you knew him." Mathilda shook her head numbly.

"You are faint. Come, sit." Kittridge guided her to a chair.

She sat down, lost to all that was about her.

"Do you have a vinaigrette with you?" he asked concernedly.

Forcing her wits to the fore, Mathilda made an effort to compose herself. "There is no need for that. I will be fine. But could you go to the cardroom and tell Lady Pennypiece I do not feel well and would like to leave?"

"Lady Pennypiece? Well, ah, yes, of course. Are you certain you shall not swoon?"

"Of course not." She gave a wan smile as proof.

"I shall return quickly," he said and strode hurriedly down the corridor.

Bartone, thought Mathilda. Of all men, it was Bartone. Bright splashes of red came to her cheeks as she thought of his kiss. How had it happened? she wondered. His face flashed to mind—those pained, fearful eyes, the tender lips. No one had ever before kissed her in such a way. Her upbringing told her it was wicked, while her heart said it could not be. Confusion swirled in ever-mounting waves. What was his purpose? Had he sought her out to discredit her? If so, how could she face Dannon and Mrs. Bertie? How could she have been so foolish?

"Dear child." Lady Pennypiece's voice intruded. "What has happened to upset you so?" She turned to Kittridge. "Please have my coach brought forward at once. And bring some brandy when you return," she ordered briskly. "Do you feel well enough to walk to the coach?" she asked Mathilda.

"Oh, I am so sorry for this trouble, my lady. Disturbing your play and . . . everything," Mathilda said, tears welling in her eyes.

"Nonsense, I was losing. Now, if I had been winning—that would have been a different tale," she teased, and was rewarded with the glint of a smile from the other. "Dry those tears before they fall," Lady Pennypiece continued, handing Mathilda her kerchief. "Drink this," she ordered as Kittridge returned and handed a glass of brandy to Mathilda.

With two gulps the brandy was down. Instantly colour flared back into Mathilda's face. "Water," she croaked. "A glass of water, please."

The countess vetoed the request. "She doesn't need it. Ruins the effects of the brandy. Come, child, the coach should be ready."

"Yes, my lady," Mathilda said meekly, and rose.

"Thank you again, Mr. Kittridge," she said. "I am certain I shall never be able to repay you for all you have done."

"You may begin by allowing me to call in the morn," he returned lightly.

"If Lady Pennypiece does not disapprove," she said, looking to her.

The countess had an odd look, but she nodded. "*Mister* Kittridge is most welcome to call."

Mathilda wondered at the cause of the look, but dismissed it as another of her ladyship's oddities, being far too upset to dwell on it. They proceeded to the doors and out to the street.

Kittridge assisted them into the coach and watched as it departed. Lady Bartone's memory had hung about the fringes of his mind since their first encounter, and his original interest was whetted by this second unusual meeting. Why was it she would be staying with Lady Pennypiece and yet not know the titled cousin? he wondered as he sauntered back to the ballroom. And if she was acceptable to Pennypiece, why had she been walking outside the Pellums'? For a simple widow in black, he noted, Lady Bartone is singularly mysterious.

CHAPTER TEN

Morning had come to full bloom before Mathilda opened her eyes, closed them, and wished for sleep to return. But consciousness, once arrived, was a tenacious visitor, and she was forced to face what she'd rather have forgotten. As she dressed, she wondered how long she could remain in her room before Lady Pennypiece insisted upon seeing her. Although the countess had not plied her with questions last night, Mathilda knew it had only been a reprieve.

If only the doll could be found and she could return to the safety of Bartone Hollows, she thought. Her hands stayed a moment on the last button of her bodice. That was the answer. She needn't stay there. Lady Pennypiece could send the doll if it was found. I could leave now—today, she thought with relief. Running to the opened wardrobe, she found her portmanteau at the bottom. Her few belongings would not take long to pack. She was in the process of folding the last petticoat when she heard steps behind her.

"You are not pleased with your room?" Lady Pennypiece asked quietly.

Mathilda spun around. "My lady . . . I . . . I . . ." she stammered.

"Is this how my generosity is to be rewarded? Running away with no word? Was I to find a simple note?" she asked curiously. "Had you thought that far?"

"My lady . . ."

"Enough. There will be no excuses." She sat upon the bed and motioned Mathilda to take the chair beside it. "I came to tell you I have ordered the servants to begin the search."

"The servants, but . . ."

"They have no idea why they are doing it. With me as mistress, they take no command as too odd. But come, I do not believe this." She waved at the portmanteau. "Has it anything to do with the doll? I cannot help you unless you tell me the problem."

Mathilda shook her head.

"In my long experience I have seen women run for but two reasons, one being that they fear their husbands, the other that they fear themselves because of a man. You have no husband, but I will not inquire as to the last," she ended.

The blood rushed to Mathilda's cheeks. "It is not the second. I love no man," she said quietly. "I simply feel it best to return to Bartone Hollows. I do not fit in here. You can write and let me know if the doll is found."

A sad sigh from the other raised Mathilda's eyes.

"So, you do not choose to trust me. I am not offended. But remember—I will listen anytime you wish to speak of it. Reconsider your decision to depart—for my sake. It would please this old woman to have you remain."

A knock sounded at the door. Upon Lady Pennypiece's call, Hollon entered bearing a silver tray with a card upon it, which she took.

Dismissing Hollon, the countess turned to Mathilda. "Kittridge has come. I will see him if you do not care to." She paused, then added, "Reconsider and stay for this one day. We should know on the morrow if the doll is to be found here."

"One day can do no harm," Mathilda answered carefully. "But that is all, my lady."

"Fine, child. Now, why don't you finish your toilet and unpack? After his assistance last night, Kittridge should at least be able to see you are yourself once more." Lady Pennypiece paused at the door. "I had not thought Kittridge one of Howard's acquaintances, but then I suppose you entertained often."

"Oh, no," Mathilda answered spontaneously. "We did little entertaining, only those in the village. I met Mr. Kittridge when I . . . when I traveled to Farnham."

The hesitation noted, Lady Pennypiece decided not to pursue it. "I will tell him you will be down directly." She nodded and was gone before Mathilda could object.

The bell below stairs in the home of Viscount Bartone rang in unsteady bursts. "Is the tonic ready?" Green asked the cook nervously.

"Just as ordered," the small man answered, placing two cups upon Green's waiting silver tray. "Don't envy him any," the cook told his assistant. "Must have been a hard night. His lordship has never risen this late. Must be nigh past two o'clock already."

Above stairs, Green entered the viscount's room quietly. He had learned to tread softly if the bell ring was not sharp and curt. Having assisted Lord Potters in putting his lordship to bed—he had arrived completely insensible——he knew his lordship's head would be worse than usual this morn. "My lord," he said quietly as he observed the closed eyes of his prostrate master.

Bartone raised an eyelid. "Do you have it?"

"Yes, my lord. Let me assist you," Green offered, setting the tray on the bedside table. His master helped to a sitting position, he placed one of the cups in his hands.

Drinking deeply, Bartone drained the cup, and

Green replaced it with the second. When it was half empty, the viscount motioned the butler to take it. He lay back, eyes closed once more. "Don't recall taking more than one before," he mumbled.

"You haven't, my lord, but considering your 'state' last eve, I thought it wise."

"Did my wife return with me?"

"Wife? Wife, my lord?" Green asked, startled from his outer calm.

"Yes, it seems we . . ." A troubled frown crept to the viscount's features.

"My lord, perhaps you had best speak with Lord Potters about the matter," Green offered nervously.

Both eyes opened and focused sharply on the butler. Bartone rubbed his hands across his face and eyes. "Get me some breakfast and send a note to Baron Potters requesting he come immediately," he demanded, sitting upright, only to lie back with a moan.

"Is this immediate enough?" Potters said cryptically, sauntering into the room.

Bartone waved Green to go. "I have a beast of a head," he groaned.

"That I don't doubt," smiled Potters.

"Did you bring me home last night, Potts?" Bartone asked casually.

"Don't you recall?"

"The last few days—weeks—are all confused. I

swore upon waking I had a . . . well, it must have been a dream."

"What did you dream?" Potters asked curiously.

The viscount rose slowly and stepped slowly to his washstand. "That I had a . . . there was this woman." He dipped his hands and rubbed his face. Drying, he turned to Potters. "Were you with me the entire evening?"

"You sound concerned," Lord Potters quipped, enjoying his friend's discomfiture.

"Were you?"

"For most of it. You were rather difficult to keep track of."

"Where did we go?"

Potters sauntered to the viscount's bed and plopped upon it. Putting his hands behind his head, he noted, "I've never known you to be concerned about where you were. What does it matter, Will?"

"I'm warning you, Potts." Bartone advanced threateningly.

Holding his arms up as if to fend him off, Potters laughed. "We only got so far as Lady Morrow's soiree. Then I brought you home."

His hand brushing through his disheveled hair, Bartone cursed. "Damme, but I was foxed!"

"Most exceptionally," the Baron noted. "But not so much so you couldn't find a woman. What I don't understand is why you picked one so out of your style."

"Out of my style," Bartone repeated. "Now, don't laugh—but I swore someone said I had a wife. I remember something happening with or about a Lady Bartone—damme! I can't sort it out, can't even recall all of it. Did anything unusual happen at the soiree?"

"Not really, except that you chose a lady who did not welcome your attentions, although I swore she was not resisting you when I first found you."

"Was there anything said about . . . about a Lady Bartone?" he asked huskily. "About my wife?"

"Wife? That's the second time you've said it. When did you wed? Think the least you could have done is tell me. You know I would not marry without telling you."

"I didn't say I had married . . ."

"Then what?"

"I don't know."

"I knew it would come, old boy. You weren't cut out to be a rake."

"Mayhaps you're right. My life has been such a . . . blur of late. I almost wonder if I didn't dream . . ."

A knock interrupted him, and Green entered. "My lord, there is a young man by the name of Pellum desiring to speak with you. He says he is a cousin and insists that it is most urgent that he speak with you about . . . Lady Bartone."

CHAPTER ELEVEN

"Mr. Pellum, I am Bartone; this is my friend, Lord Potters." The viscount greeted his visitor curtly. "What is this about Lady Bartone?"

"My mother, Sir Bartone's sister, believes this woman calling herself Lady Bartone is nothing more than a tart—a lightskirt, from the muslin set . . ."

"I believe you've made your point," Bartone cut him off. "This Lady Bartone is Sir Bartone's wife?"

"That is what she claims, but only to get uncle's money. That's what Mother says."

Relief, yet concern, showed on Bartone's face.

"Don't you see, my lord, his estate is rightfully ours—yours, and of course Lady Pennypiece's also. Uncle Howard left no heirs," Pellum protested.

"Wait. You want me to help take Sir Bartone's estate from his wife because there were no children?" the viscount asked angrily, thinking of a poor old woman.

"You don't understand, my lord. It isn't as you think. She is of my age, a pauper's daughter who snared Uncle Howard when he was in his dotage, from what Mother has learned. The woman not only dared to visit my mother but has actually called on Lady Pennypiece. Mother was certain Aunt Netta would support us in this, but she has actually taken the tart in," he ended contemptuously.

"Lady Bartone is staying with Lady Pennypiece?" the viscount asked.

"Yes. Why, she even took her to Lady Morrow's soiree the past eve. I left as soon as they arrived," Pellum blustered.

"Green, show Mr. Pellum out. Have my phaeton brought to the door. Potts, come along. Good day, Pellum."

Kittridge rose as Mathilda entered the morning room. "How good to see you, Lady Bartone," he greeted her, "and how reassuring to see you fully recovered."

"I must thank you once again . . ." she began.

"Let it be forgotten. Lady Pennypiece was just telling me this is your first visit to London. Have you enjoyed the sights the city has to offer?" he asked as he escorted her to a seat beside her ladyship.

"I have not had time to see much."

"Then we must change that. I am free the remainder of the day and should be pleased to show you some of the more prominent sights."

"I think that an excellent idea. It would be good for you," Lady Pennypiece said, giving Mathilda's hand a squeeze. "Do not say you are not tempted."

"Well, if you would accompany us . . ."

"Faddle, I have appointments I must keep. You do not need a chaperon. Go and enjoy yourself," she urged.

"I will be happy to go," Mathilda said, turning back to Kittridge. A new thought occurred to her, and her smile faded. "But this is my only day gown. I did not see the need of bringing much with me."

"It is most charming," Kittridge assured her gallantly, seeing the distress in her large, kind eyes rather than the black bombazine, Mathilda's second-best dress and sadly lacking in style.

"Off with you," her ladyship ordered happily.

"You are certain?" Mathilda asked. "Could I not be of some help to you?"

"You would find a day with me boring, child. Go on."

"I will fetch my wrap and bonnet," Mathilda told Kittridge, and hurried off.

"You have a most attractive sister-in-law—much like yourself," he commented to Lady Pennypiece.

"Yes, I would say she is as naive and unsuspecting as I was many years ago, *Mister* Kittridge."

A slightly foolish yet pained grin came to his face.

"She is not of the seasoned *haut ton*," Lady

Pennypiece said to him. "I do not think she will look upon deception kindly or without suspicion."

"I have not sought to . . ." Kittridge began.

"Knowing you, I must admit to some surprise. My advice, however, is to rectify the illusion before someone else does," Countess Pennypiece warned him.

Light, tripping steps told them of Mathilda's return.

"You look lovely, my dear," her ladyship said, noting the colour in Mathilda's face. "Enjoy yourself but do not overdo. Return Lady Bartone at a sensible hour, Mr. Kittridge, for we go to the opera this eve," she added, turning to the gentleman.

"Perhaps I may escort you?" He glanced from Lady Pennypiece to Mathilda.

Mathilda dropped her eyes, but not before she saw the twinkle in Lady Pennypiece's look and knew she had been entrapped.

"Of course you may," the crafty countess smiled. "Till this eve, and recall that I dislike the crush," she noted as she left the room.

"Yes, my lady," Kittridge bowed after her. Turning back to Mathilda, he asked, "What shall we see first? Shall it be St. Paul's or the Tower?" He offered his arm.

"Oh, could we climb to St. Paul's Whispering Gallery?" Mathilda asked, clapping her hands in delight. "And of course we must take in Madame Tussaud's." Eagerness brought a lovely rose hue to her features. "Oh, there is so much to see, so many places I have read of. Bartone spoke of so much that is here."

Kittridge glanced at her. Did she mean her husband or the viscount? Did it matter?

"Pardon, my lord, but I said no one goes further without her ladyship's permission," Hollon said menacingly.

"I am her cousin," Bartone swore. "She will not wish me put off."

"Easy, Will," Potters urged.

"I can announce myself," Bartone said, taking a step around Hollon.

The huge man took hold of the viscount and seated him soundly in a chair. "You will wait, your lordship," he said, tightening his grip on Bartone's shoulder.

"This is ridiculous," burst from the viscount as he attempted to free himself.

"Go and request Lady Pennypiece to see us," Lord Potters told Hollon, laying a hand on Bartone's free shoulder. "The viscount shall remain here."

Reluctantly, the huge hand released its hold. With a distrustful backward glance at the glaring viscount, he went to do as bid.

Shrugging free of Potters's hand, Bartone asked, "Why did you do that, Potts? I was capable of . . ."

"Of getting thrown out, Will. What is wrong with you?"

Bartone ignored the question as he straightened his jacket and cravat.

"This way, my lords," Hollon said, reappearing. He showed them to a small, book-lined room which Lady Pennypiece used for an office. "Her ladyship will be with you soon. See you don't bother anything." With a warning nod, he shut the door.

"Admirable servant," Potters noted lightly.

"Bah," returned the viscount. "As odd as his mistress."

"Sit down. What is it we seek here? Did you believe what that fellow said?"

"Couldn't I simply be calling upon an aged cousin to inquire after her? You are the one who says I must have more feeling for others," Bartone said, shrugging off the question.

"Aged, but not dulled. Mother plays whist with Lady Pennypiece and always comes off the worst for it. She's not a bad player, either. Gives me a rough go of it at times."

"To what do I owe the honour of this visit, my lords?" Lady Pennypiece asked, her expressionless features hiding her excitement.

Both men rose and bowed.

"Come, my lords, you have arrived at a most inconvenient moment; I do not have much time to spare."

"The fact that Lady Bartone is staying with you

was brought to my attention this morn . . ." the viscount began.

"Ah, Richard has reached you at last. He has been trying for several days, you know."

"Is what he says true?"

"How am I to know what he has said to you?" Lady Pennypiece asked innocently.

"I was given the impression that Lady Bartone is a young woman—not much past twenty."

"I suppose that to be true. Not an unlucky thing to be guilty of, I might add." She winked at Potters.

"But your brother was past eighty."

"Also true."

"This does not make you suspicious of her motives for marrying him or for coming to you now?" Bartone demanded.

His tone stiffened Lady Pennypiece's back. "I know them exactly. If you desire to learn them, I suggest you speak to Lady Bartone. Good day, my lords."

"I will see her now," the viscount commanded, following the countess into the corridor.

"Unfortunately, she is out at the moment."

"When will she be returning?" he asked sharply.

"It matters not if you do not improve your manners, my lord," her ladyship said calmly. "Do not call again until you do. Hollon."

The huge butler came into the corridor.

"Show his lordship out."

Hollon advanced a step.

Swearing, Bartone turned on his heel and stalked out.

Edging his way into the corridor, Lord Potters bowed to Lady Pennypiece, keeping one eye on Hollon. "So good of you to see us, my lady. Good day to you." He bowed again and hurried after Bartone. "What was the meaning of that scene?" burst from him as he climbed into the phaeton.

For an answer he was thrown back against the plush blue velvet cushion of the viscount's smart phaeton. Its black wheels with blue spokes whirred as Bartone put the whip to his team. Skilled as a four-in-hand, he managed the phaeton through the teeming afternoon traffic while Potters felt the end was surely come.

When Bartone halted the team, his friend shakily descended to the ground. "Will, I have called you friend from the cradle. For this reason, I have borne much, but no more—not unless you manage to curb whatever has you acting like a madman. You aren't the man I once knew, and I am not the fool you think."

"I'm the only friend you have, Potts. What will you do without me?" Bartone asked, the effect of the evening and his anger still evident.

Lord Potters drew himself up, straightened his spectacles, and said sadly, "Isn't that rather backward? What are you going to do without me?"

CHAPTER TWELVE

"Did you have an enjoyable time with Mr. Kittridge?" Lady Pennypiece asked, encountering Mathilda as they both walked toward the supper room.

"A most pleasant day, my lady. St. Paul's was magnificent! And we did climb the entire way to the Whispering Gallery."

"I didn't know how fortunate I was to have been occupied elsewhere," her ladyship quipped.

Some of the sparkle left Mathilda at these words as she thought of the gowns she had found in her room upon her return. "You were rather busy, weren't you?" she said slowly, unsure how to approach the problem.

"From that tone, I believe you are ready to call me Netta, or Aunt Nettie if you prefer, and I shall call you Mathilda when I like. Now let us dine, and then we shall discuss my work, as you say. Tell me, what did you think of Madame Tussaud's?" she asked, turning the subject in a direction she preferred.

"We can speak of that after you tell me the result of this day's search. My reason for coming here has not been lost in the pleasure of the day," Mathilda noted, becoming serious.

"With Kittridge's interest in you, I wonder that you are concerned. He would be a good catch," Lady Pennypiece said pointedly.

"Mr. Kittridge is a very kind gentleman and most . . . pleasant, but I came to London not for a husband but for a doll. Has it been found?"

"A doll certainly is less trouble than a husband, but somehow I don't feel it would be as satisfying," Lady Pennypiece noted artlessly. "Do not frown so—causes wrinkles. The doll has not been found, but do not despair. In the morn I will send some trusted servants to search my country house. There is a greater chance that I have it there, for London did not appeal to me when I was first wed. Now to our meal."

Dinner passed quickly as Lady Pennypiece drew out all that Mathilda had observed. She found her judgment of the young woman confirmed. Mathilda spoke not only of the glories she had seen but also of the harsher realities.

Rising from the meal, Lady Pennypiece answered Mathilda's question about Londoners' dining habits with "Many think it foolish to dine so early, but I find that some of the operas require a degree of stamina only food can provide. Let us dress. Mr. Kittridge will be calling for us soon. Shall I send one of my maids to assist you in your toilet?"

"I am dressed," Mathilda returned, smoothing the skirts of her black silk. "If this is unsuitable, I shall remain here."

Countess Pennypiece raised her quizzing glass to her eye. "That gown was fashionable seasons ago."

"Nevertheless, I will wear it this eve. It will have to do," Mathilda answered stubbornly.

"I believe Howard has bequeathed his obstinacy to you. Now don't be foolish."

"The lovely gowns I found . . ." A look of dismay filled Mathilda's features. "I could not help admiring them, but I cannot accept them, and I certainly cannot afford to buy them."

"Proud, eh? Well, the truth is I was feeling guilty for having never sent a wedding gift. Widow's weeds are not exactly what one thinks of for such a gift, but then neither am I a usual person."

"They could hardly be called weeds, my lady." She saw Lady Pennypiece's stern expression. "I mean, Aunt Nettie, I am not knowledgeable about prices or materials such as they are made from, but they must be very expensive. It would not be right for me to accept them."

"You force me to admit it all, but promise you shall tell no one. An old woman such as I has little more than pride with which to face the world." She moved closer. "I have mentioned Beau Brummel's words to me. Now, most think I care not what anyone says about my toilet." Her wave encompassed the elaborate wig and full-skirted gown. "But it is my mark. I cannot have you challenging it."

"Challenge? Why I would never," protested Mathilda.

"How can it be thought otherwise? It is known my brother was not impoverished. Why should his wife appear in London in gowns two or three seasons past if not to attempt to displace me?" She bowed her head and dabbed at her eyes, managing, however, a peek at Mathilda to assess the effect of her words.

"Truly, I did not think such a thing. These are my only gowns."

"I know that, my dear, but others will not believe it. Accept the gowns for my sake. Let me end my years as *the* eccentric," she ended, sighing sadly.

Suspicion, followed by a grin, appeared on Mathilda's face. "You would coax the honey from a bee with it never having seen a flower," she laughed. "To please you, I will wear one of the gowns," she conceded, "but I shall not take it with me when I depart on the morrow."

"On the morrow? Ah, yes. Do not dillydally

now. I wish to see how you look properly gowned. It is fortunate your hair style flatters," she told Mathilda bluntly. "Off with you."

The oval mirror of the wardrobe reflected a stranger to Mathilda's eyes. She had chosen a high-waisted, sleeveless gown of black satin with a sleeved overdress of black gossamer silk, upon which a band of classic design had been patterned, with white seed pearls at the hem, across the bodice, and at the edge of the sleeves. The high waistline and soft draping of the rich silk material was admirably suited to Mathilda's form. With her dark-blond hair drawn smoothly back, then braided and pinned as a crown atop her head, her features took on an appealing fragility. Her hazel eyes, reflecting the black of the gown, darkened enticingly. She turned slowly before the high oval mirror. "I must be bewitched. Oh, what would Mrs. Bertie say if she saw this?" Her smile dimmed at the thought, for without the doll her happiness and that of those depending upon her was only momentary.

"My lady," the small voice of the upstairs maid called from beyond the door. "Lady Pennypiece wishes you to come to the salon. Mr. Kittridge has arrived."

"Tell her ladyship I am coming," Mathilda answered. Taking one last look, she spoke softly to her reflection, "What a vain creature you are, after all. But this moment is brief and we are going to enjoy it."

Mathilda tried to suppress the excitement she felt as she halted just outside the salon's doors. Her reflection had given her an air of confidence, and she entered with the grace of the best of the *haut ton*, rendering the entrance charming by breaking into soft laughter as she halted before Lady Pennypiece.

The countess motioned with her quizzing glass for Mathilda to turn about for inspection. A half circle brought her face-to-face with Kittridge, who gave her an elaborate bow, stepped forward, took her hand, and kissed it.

"Excellent, m . . . my lady," he said to Lady Pennypiece, not taking his eyes from Mathilda.

Under his admiring stare her colour rose even higher, as she could not help but think of the countess's words about him.

"I am sorry to disturb you, Kittridge, but we must go . . ."

"You know I hate the late crush," he finished, turning with a smile to Lady Pennypiece.

Mathilda went to the old woman as she rose, opened her lips to thank her, then impulsively hugged her, kissing her cheek.

"My dear Mathilda, you must take care," Lady Pennypiece said gruffly. "Such a creation"—she patted her elaborately curled wig—"must be treated with care. Let us go—let us go."

"Certainly, my lady," Kittridge said, offering an arm to each. "With two of the most beautiful women in London in my company, I will be the most envied man."

"Of course," Lady Pennypiece replied matter-of-factly, her eyes twinkling mischievously. "My presence almost insures you an uninterrupted eve with Mathilda. It should be ample opportunity to convince her of your virtues." Ignoring the glare from Mathilda, she walked away from the pair.

"We had better follow. She'll take the coach and leave us," laughed Kittridge, putting Mathilda once more at ease.

"I am not certain it would not be wiser to let her," she responded softly, but quickly stepped ahead as she saw a gleam of concurrence in his eye.

Applause rose in a wave and then slowly subsided as the curtains were drawn at the end of the first act. Kittridge nudged Mathilda and nodded at Lady Pennypiece. The old woman sat perfectly upright and sound asleep.

Her eyes slowly opened as the noise of the audience grew. Blinking, she spied the two grinning at her. "Thought I was sleeping, eh?" she snorted. "Merely getting the fullest measure from the music." With a tap of her fan on Kittridge's arm she ordered, "See to some refreshments for us."

"Lady Bartone, would you care to walk with me as I attend this royal command?"

"No, she would not—now off with you."

He rose and bowed. "Be wary," he winked at Mathilda. "When she is charming, she is most dangerous."

Mathilda wondered at the cavalier manner with which Kittridge treated Lady Pennypiece and her acceptance of it.

"I must put an end to his insubordinate behaviour," the countess spoke, seeing the question on the other's face. "Young bucks are lax in their respect for their elders these days."

Raucous laughter joined with protesting jeers turned both women to the boxes across the way. A woman in a diaphanous gown was leaning over the edge of one of the boxes, emptying a bottle of champagne on those below. The men and women in the box with her were laughing and urging her on. A man whose back had been turned to them staggered upright and grabbed her. He collapsed into a chair, pulling her onto his lap. She put the bottle to his lips, and he drank while the wine ran down his waistcoat.

"Hrrumph," snorted Lady Pennypiece, lowering her quizzing glass.

"Who are they?" Mathilda asked, still staring.

"That is Viscount Bartone's box, and I would

imagine those with him are of Harriet Wilson's set—the worst profligates in London," she answered, frowning. "The one with the lightskirt on his lap is our cousin—Bartone."

Mathilda, with an indrawn breath, turned her eyes back instantly, but she could not see him, as he was now kissing the occupant of his lap enthusiastically.

"Lady Pennypiece, so good to see you. Isn't the performance excellent this eve," a large matronly woman spoke as she entered their box, followed by a bespectacled, nervous young man. "You know my son, Daniel."

Lord Potters bowed, his apprehension at this meeting apparent.

"May I present Lady Bartone, Lady Potters," the countess introduced them. "Now, Helen, leave the young ones to themselves. Come, sit. Tell me, what have you heard lately of Mrs. Fitzherbert?"

"Would you care to be seated, my lord?" Mathilda asked, seeing she was on her own. "My lord?" she repeated when he did not answer.

"Excuse me, Lady Bartone," Potters apologized, taking his eyes from Bartone's box and sitting.

"Do you know Viscount Bartone?" she asked timidly.

"Well acquainted with him. Yes, rather well," he said. "A dastardly shame, such a waste, but you mustn't judge him too harshly."

"Judge him? My lord, what reason would I have to do so?" Mathilda protested. "I am not acquainted with his lordship."

"No? Well," Potters looked closely at her. "Thought I'd seen you with Will for some reason. But whatever you say," he hastened to add. "Kittridge," he said in greeting, rising as the other returned. "Good eve."

"Lady Potters," Kittridge acknowledged her presence, "what an elegant turban you wear this eve. It will soon be the rage among all the dowagers."

Highly pleased, Lady Potters nodded and smiled before plunging ahead with the latest *on dit* with Lady Pennypiece. The porter, who had followed Kittridge, served champagne to all as Kittridge took a seat beside Mathilda.

"An excellent speech yesterday, Daniel. We need more men willing to support the abolition issue."

"Thank you, Kittridge, but it will be a futile effort without a majority." A loud burst of laughter drew his eyes to Bartone's box. "I had hoped to convince Will to join us—Viscount Bartone," he amended, seeing Mathilda's questioning look. "But I am beginning to fear it is hopeless."

"I have heard he had a difficult time of it in the Indies—was actually in the hands of the French for a time. Perhaps he will come about yet," offered Kittridge.

Potters shrugged sadly. "We should not be boring you, Lady Bartone. Are you enjoying your visit?" he asked, to change the direction of the conversation.

Forcing herself to pay attention, Mathilda took part in the light, bantering conversation. But as the second act was about to begin, and Lady and Lord Potters took their leave, her eyes strayed to Bartone's box.

The viscount was looking directly at her. As their gazes met and locked, Mathilda felt her pulse surge. Kittridge touched her arm, and she turned to him reluctantly. "Are you quite comfortable? This act is rather long," he inquired.

"Yes, of course. Thank you," she answered vaguely. Her eyes swung back immediately, but Bartone was gone.

CHAPTER THIRTEEN

Departure, Mathilda soon discovered, was not a word recognized by the countess, at least not if it pertained to Mathilda's return to Bartone Hollows. Persuaded to await the return of the servants sent to search Lady Pennypiece's country estate, Pennywise, Mathilda found herself taking part in the regular whirlwind of the *haut ton*'s London activities.

The countess enthusiastically launched Mathilda on an endless round of morning calls, shopping expeditions, afternoon drives in the park, and evenings at cotillions, soirees, the theatre, and the opera. Squired by Kittridge, escorted by Lord Potters, and always with Lady Pennypiece carefully on the fringe, Mathilda grew in confidence and poise. Only brief glimpses and chance encounters with Viscount Bartone, always darkly brooding and disapproving, disturbed her.

That the encounters were by chance Mathilda began to doubt one evening just two weeks after her arrival in London at Lady Potters's ball. After having gone through the receiving line, she and Mr. Kittridge saw Lady Pennypiece to the cardroom. The first set of country dances was forming when they entered the ballroom and Kittridge insisted Mathilda take part with him. Being uncertain of her steps, she was glad when it came to an end. She hastily refused his offer for the second set, insisting instead that he ask a young lady he had introduced her to earlier in the week and had seemed partial to. After strenuous assurances that she would come to no harm left alone, Kittridge heeded her words. He was barely out of sight when a familiar voice drew Mathilda's attention.

"Lady Mathilda," Lord Potters said, walking up to her and giving a bow. "I presumed Kittridge was monopolizing your dance card."

"I sent him off to dance with Lady Alice, Lady Glashow's daughter," Mathilda laughed gently. "I do think he appreciates her looks."

"Half the men in London dangle after her," Potters agreed. "But let us dance if you are free. I would be a poor host to let you stand about alone."

"If you wouldn't mind, I would rather walk about. You could tell me how your work in Parliament is coming."

"Would you really care to hear of that? Not the sort of thing most women take a fancy for," he replied, somewhat surprised.

"Sir Bartone often spoke with me about Parliament. He was an MP much longer than a knight and never lost interest in either house. Right up to his last days he encouraged me to read to him the reports on the proceedings from the papers," Mathilda began. "He said the saddest thing was that so many lords neglected their duty by never taking their seats."

"Quite right there," Potters answered, a sad frown coming to his face. He fell silent as they walked, and began adjusting his spectacles.

Mathilda had noticed the look and action before. It had come to her that it was Lord Potters's reaction whenever he saw or thought of Viscount Bartone. "You worry a good deal about him, don't you?" she quietly voiced the question that came to her.

"Rather much, yes. Habit, you know." He stopped and gave Mathilda an assessing stare. "How did you know? No, you needn't answer that." He began walking once more. "Would you mind if we talked about him?"

"Of course not. It must be very difficult to see an old friend slowly destroying himself. Pardon me, I did not mean to become so personal. Lady Pennypiece told me you two were good friends."

The sad smile he gave assured her no insult had been taken. "Destroy? Yes, I suppose that is the correct word, although no one seems to view it that way. I tried to help him, to steer him away from those who lured him to more drink, more women. Everything I suggested only seemed to plunge him deeper. Finally, I decided the only way I could help him was to step away," Lord Potters ended, his words filled with anguish.

Seeking to comfort him, Mathilda said, "You did the right thing. As long as he had you as a crutch, he could not help himself. Sir Bartone always said no one can redeem a man but the man himself."

"Yes, but he was my crutch also for so many years. It was not until he went to the Indies for his father that I had to stand on my own. At times it seems so cowardly for me to desert him now."

"Your own words prove the wisdom of your decision. Would you be as you now are if he had never left? You did not desert him." She paused and forced Potters to look at her. "There is nothing else you could honourably do."

"It still haunts me, though. I see him watch me cross a street or chat at a cotillion and he gives no sign of recognition, just stares accusingly. Will wasn't always like that. I wish you could have known him before he went to the Indies." A smile came to Potters's face as he reminisced. "Some say he was too wild by far, but I never saw him harm anyone. He got me out of scrape after scrape—and into too many to count." He laughed softly.

Mathilda smiled also, visualizing what the

handsome Bartone must have been like as a lad. The vision was slowly overpowered by the haunted, accusing appeal she had seen on that moonlit terrace at Lady Morrow's. His face appeared so real, she shook her head, then gasped, for Bartone stood before them.

"Lord Potters . . . Lady Bartone," he greeted them stiffly.

"I'm glad you came, Will," Potters said, extending his hand.

"I was surprised you were able to convince your mother I was socially fit to come," Bartone returned, ignoring the gesture.

Dropping his hand to his side, Potters ignored the words, saying, "You know you are welcome here, Will, at any time, for any reason."

The two men's eyes met. Bartone's dropped first. He turned to Mathilda. "Lady Bartone, would you do the honour of dancing with me?"

"I am sorry, my lord, but Lord Potters and I . . ." she began.

"Never mind, Lady Mathilda, we can continue our conversation another time. I really must see to Mother's guests. I hope to speak with you later, Will." He bowed to them both and walked away.

"Lady Bartone?" The viscount stood, awaiting her response.

There being no polite escape, Mathilda nodded acceptance. Her heart lurched as she took Bartone's arm and followed his lead to the ballroom. Neither spoke during that brief walk, nor as they assumed their places in the forming allemande.

Mathilda could feel his eyes watching her every move; her colour rose higher. Raising her eyes, she saw an appeal quickly concealed behind a guarded expression. As they danced, he offered no conversation, and she began to wonder at his purpose in dancing with her. The music drifted to silence and conversation broke out all around them as gentlemen took ladies to their mothers or claimed their partners for the next dance. At one side, the viscount stared down at Mathilda, her hand still held in his.

She longed to speak but could find no words. Panic began to well within as she felt her pulse begin to hammer. Relief plainly showed upon her features when she heard her name called out.

Bartone glanced to see who it was that had spoken and paled slightly beneath his tan as Mathilda warmly welcomed Kittridge. His look became shielded, as if to hide a hurt. He raised Mathilda's hands to his lips, abruptly bowed, and stalked out of sight.

Some instinct urged Mathilda to call out to him, to run after him and prevent his leaving, but she quelled it sternly, turning to Kittridge with a bright, false smile and the inkling of a tear in her eye. He was gentleman enough not to notice.

* * *

"If you insist, I will take along the little upstairs maid, Mary," Mathilda said, barely concealing her disgust at the suggestion. "I simply wish to walk for a time in the fresh air as I did at the Hollows."

"You do look a bit peaked this morn. Was Lady Potters's ball too much? Never mind, the morning air will revive your spirits, but would you like me to send our regrets to Lady Devonshire about this evening?" Lady Pennypiece asked as she raised her cup of tea to her lips.

"That is not necessary, Aunt Nettie. You know you are looking forward to it," she replied, tying her bonnet atop her honeybrown curls. "Now, I am only going to be out a short time," Mathilda said, brushing the countess's cheek with a kiss.

"But I haven't called Mary," objected Lady Pennypiece as Mathilda left the morning room.

"No, I recalled how you told me becoming a widow enabled you to do without a bothersome chaperon," Mathilda called back. She hastened out the door Hollon held open for her before Lady Pennypiece could reply.

At first Mathilda strode firmly along the street, indifferent to all about her. But soon she noticed the odd glances she was attracting and slowed her steps to a more ladylike pace. The casual amble left her mind freer to roam, and it went immediately to Viscount Bartone, who was occupying an increasing and alarming portion of her thoughts. Mathilda did not know what to make of his actions, especially of last night at Lady Potters's ball. Worse, she was puzzled by her own reaction. What is it about the man? she asked herself. He does not have the gentlemanly manners of Mr. Kittridge or the kindness of Lord Potters. He drinks too much, does nothing useful with his time, and still . . .

Having become deeply involved with her own thoughts, Mathilda did not realize her steps had quickened and that she was not paying attention to those before her. That she should have been more observant was brought home with a resounding thud, as she walked solidly into an approaching gentleman.

To keep from falling, the man grabbed Mathilda, releasing her as they both regained their balance. Both began immediate apologies, only to halt as they recognized each other. Mathilda was dismayed and yet somehow gladdened to see it was Viscount Bartone who was gazing down at her with a suspicious frown.

"My lord, I beg your pardon. I'm afraid I was not minding my steps," she apologized. She blushed fiercely as he stood silent. "I'll just be on my way," Mathilda went on awkwardly.

"I will walk with you," Bartone finally spoke. "I was meaning to call on you this morn."

Mathilda looked up at the tanned, cleanly chiseled features of the viscount's face and couldn't help but think that a smile would suit it much more than the scowl which now darkened it.

"Why are you walking alone?" he demanded suddenly. "Can't old Pennypiece spare a maid for you?"

"I chose to walk alone," Mathilda snapped back, turning from him and walking forward. *Now, why did I do that?* She scolded herself at the unusual burst of temper on her part. Footsteps sounded at her side. A quick glance showed the viscount matching her pace, step for step. When she halted, he did. When she went forward, he followed. Finally she stopped and confronted him. "What is it, my lord?" she asked, irritation in her voice and face alike.

For the first time a smile lit Bartone's face. "I was wondering if you would go riding with me this afternoon."

"I do not ride, my lord," she answered crisply.

"Then I shall bring my phaeton," he returned. "Good day. I shall be calling at five."

With open-mouthed surprise, Mathilda watched the neatly dressed form stride away from her. "But I . . ." she began, then stamped her foot and turned back toward Golden Square.

Bartones, she thought angrily. *They are all of the same cast—highhanded, self-interested . . .* her thoughts softened. . . . *and with obnoxiously winning ways.*

CHAPTER FOURTEEN

"But why are you going with Bartone?" Lady Pennypiece demanded. "You know what we have been hearing of the man. He's not drawn a sober breath in the last two weeks."

"He was not foxed this morn, nor last eve for that matter," Mathilda replied. "Besides, he used that Bartone charm you employ so wisely at times."

"Which is?"

"Not giving me time to answer," Mathilda said, trying to suppress her smile. "I mean no insult, Aunt Nettie. Has it not appeared odd for me not to be seen in Bartone's company? Family ties urge some acquaintanceship."

"Not with the likes of him. I thought you were to go with Kittridge," Lady Pennypiece groused.

"I have sent a note to him explaining how awkward it would be to have both arrive. I have been seen in Mr. Kittridge's company too frequently since I arrived. Tongues will carry tales, as you know."

"What of it, eh? I thought you were fond of him," the countess said gruffly.

"I am, and ever so grateful, but . . . but it is not fair to him."

"Hrrumph. Well, if you insist, I suppose no harm can come from one outing. But I told that young Bartone not to call again until he learned better manners, and I mean to stand by that."

"What do you mean?"

"That young buck appeared here the day after you arrived, demanding to see you as if you were an upstairs maid. Hollon gave him a lesson," she ended, nodding briskly.

"Not in deportment, I gather," Mathilda noted skeptically. "Did the viscount happen to say why he wished to see me?"

"No, only that Richard Pellum had been to see him. Sometimes I feel like disinheriting that nephew of mine. Too like his mother for me."

"Calm yourself, Aunt Nettie. Mr. Pellum has been very polite when we've encountered him."

"He daren't be otherwise. Now be careful of young Bartone. I don't trust him, nor his reasons for this sudden friendliness."

"My lord, pardon the interruption," Green said, entering after knocking, "but Mr. Pellum is insisting he speak with you immediately."

"Tell him I'll see him when I have finished and not before," Bartone said, scowling at the thought of his skeletal cousin. "Continue, Mr. Nettles," he demanded impatiently of the smallish man before him.

"As I was saying, your lordship, there is not much to be learned of the lady. Few are acquainted with her in London. All of Lady Pennypiece's servants and merchants who do know her, speak highly of her manners and kindnesses." He brushed back a wisp of hair that had fallen forward. "There is one odd thing, though," Nettles noted. "It seems since the lady arrived, the household has been turned from top to bottom in the search for a doll."

"A doll? I do not pay you to learn about dolls. What has it to do with the matter?" scoffed the viscount.

"Well, your lordship, in my business you have to have a feel for things, and my bones tell me this doll is important to the lady."

Bartone returned to his chair. He drummed his fingers on the desk top. "So you have learned nothing to the lady's discredit?"

"No, my lord."

"I want you to go immediately to the village of Horley. Learn what you can without arousing too much suspicion. I want no mention made of my name." He paused, and Nettles nodded. "From there, go to Farnham and see what you can learn of the Pellums. Be thorough, but make haste," Bartone ended rising. "Green will show you out."

"Good day, my lord. I will call upon you as soon as I return," Nettles said, giving a curt bow.

Turning from him, Bartone stared at the wall of book-filled shelves before him. *This time I must be certain*, he thought, *before I commit myself*.

A beautiful, delicately featured face slipped through the bars his mind had erected and confronted him. Bitterness flooded back. "You fool," he swore harshly at himself.

"My lord, pardon. What have I done?" The fear-struck voice of Richard Pellum sounded.

Facing the white-faced vulture, Bartone demanded, "What is it you want?"

"My lord . . . I . . . I . . . Mother, that is . . . wishes to know if we can . . . if you will join us in our suit to get what is ours from Uncle Howard's estate . . . join in our effort to have that woman disinherited, completely disinherited." Pellum spoke in quivering tones.

"What concrete evidence do you have? Do you think she killed the old man?" barked the viscount.

"No, oh, no, my lord." Pellum backed away from the violence reflected in Bartone's face. "I will come another time, my lord . . ."

"No. Sit," Bartone commanded, taking his seat behind his desk once more. "I want to hear all you know of Lady Bartone."

Quailing, Pellum took the chair the viscount indicated. "There is not much I know of the . . . lady—personally that is," Richard began fearfully.

"Why did she call at Farnham?"

"That does seem harmless enough an act, I suppose," Pellum replied nervously. "She brought a small chest of childhood mementoes that belonged to my mother. Said she had found them in the attics at the Hollows and thought that Mother would like to have them. Was a very strange thing for her to do, traveling for such a reason when Mother had refused to even answer her letters or go to Uncle Howard's funeral."

"You believe she came only to return the chest?"

"You must remember that Mother was not at home when Lady Bartone called. When she returned just a few moments later, she was incensed at discovering the tart in her own parlour and ordered her out. A lady does not speak to that sort of person," he ended righteously.

"And your mother is that sort?" Bartone waved aside Pellum's startled reaction. "So nothing was learned but that she wished to return some worthless toys. I imagine your mother managed to keep those. Tell me, did anyone think to wait and see if she was going to offer to share the estate?" A hint of a sardonic smile appeared at Pellum's alarm. "Nothing else was spoken of before your mother returned?" he asked hopefully, cursing Mrs. Pellum's hasty action.

"Just some small talk, some nonsense about Doll in Red," Richard answered, shrugging, still preoccupied with Bartone's previous question.

"Doll in Red?"

The viscount's tone caught Pellum's attention. "It's not important, my lord. Some doll Mother had as a child. Wish she hadn't been reminded of it—had to hear how Aunt Netta stole off with it, and all that folderol. Utter nonsense."

"Yes, of course," the viscount agreed. "Did she ask to see the doll?"

"I really couldn't say, my lord. She mentioned something about seeing it in a portrait at the Hollows. Imagine she took a fancy to it. Dropped the subject when my sister told her Aunt Netta had it."

The viscount drummed his fingers pensively for a moment. "You will have to excuse me, Pellum. Tell your mother I have taken the matter under consideration," he said in dismissal.

"Thank you, my lord," Pellum said, much relieved. "Thank you." He bowed, then waited, uncertain if he should take his leave. "The business of the doll is absurd, you know," he mumbled awkwardly, seeking something to say as he backed to the door.

Bartone looked up as the door clicked shut behind Pellum. *What was the nonsense about the* doll? Doll in Red. Would it be a red doll, a doll dressed in red, or what? he thought. *It does seem Nettles was correct in its being important. Appears the lady came to London hoping to find it here—but why? What is the importance of the doll?*

CHAPTER FIFTEEN

A glowering warning etched itself over Hollon's face upon opening the door and seeing Viscount Bartone.

"Good day, Hollon. Tell Lady Pennypiece I have come to offer an apology. Please give her these on my behalf," the viscount said, handing a large spray of yellow roses to the butler.

"Wait here, yer lordship. I'll see what her ladyship says," Hollon told him, taking the flowers. "What about the others?" he asked, nodding at the posy of babypink roses Bartone still held.

"I'll keep these," the viscount answered.

"You just wait here, then—no foolishness." The huge man grunted and stalked off.

Bartone glanced at the posy he held. Would she like the roses? Perhaps they were not to her taste. Would she go with him or have some ready excuse waiting? Perhaps she had already left. His mind raced through the possibilities. With an oath, he quelled his nervousness with his cold skepticism. *If she is what I think, nothing will prevent her from going with me*, he told himself.

"Come this way, yer lordship," Hollon called from the foot of the stairs. "A shame yer forgiven," he muttered. "Wouldn't have minded a little to do with ye." With that he took the viscount to the third-floor room where Mathilda had first seen Lady Pennypiece. Announcing him, Hollon withdrew.

The hominess of the scene made Bartone hesitate to enter. Large comfortable chairs, each with its own small table and lamp beside it, were clustered in front of the long span of windows, now draped with a sheer muslin of a warm yellow shade. At the sound of the viscount's name, Mathilda had looked up from her needlepoint with a warm smile.

"Enter, young man," Lady Pennypiece commanded. "You have something to say?"

"I had hoped the flowers would speak for me, my lady." He bowed before the countess. "There is no home they could grace with more honour than yours. Please accept my humble apologies for my behaviour and allow me the permission to present these"—he brought the posy of pink roses from behind his back—"to Lady Bartone as an expression of regret at my tardiness in calling upon her and offering my sympathies at the loss of her husband."

At these words Lady Pennypiece raised her

quizzing glass to her eye, peering sharply at the viscount, her distrust growing. Seeing he was enduring the inspection without flinching, she grudgingly said, "Lady Bartone does as she pleases, accepts what she wishes to as she sees fit."

"Lady Bartone." He extended his hand, offering the posy. "I do hope this will please you."

"They are beautiful," she answered, rising and laying aside her needlepoint. "How could they fail to please anyone? You are very kind." Her hand brushed his as she accepted the flowers; their eyes met.

"Is the day as pleasant as it appears from this room?" Lady Pennypiece asked.

"Yes, my lady," Bartone answered, watching Mathilda lower her eyes from his in confusion. "Perhaps you would care to come with us?" he offered.

"I think not. You young bloods are not as careful of a team as you should be."

"I have my phaeton at the door, Lady Bartone. Will you come? I promise to take care in driving and I dare not leave the team with my tiger for too long, as they are fresh and tend to be nervous."

"Go on, child," Lady Pennypiece answered Mathilda's unspoken question.

"It will only take a moment for me to fetch my bonnet," Mathilda told Bartone. She hurried to the door. "Thank you," she said, turning back to him with a heart-lifting smile.

He nodded, returning the smile and watching Mathilda as she ran to the stairs.

"What are you up to, young man?" Lady Pennypiece asked with her usual curtness after Mathilda had gone.

"My lady, what can you mean?" Bartone asked quietly, facing her squarely.

"I'll not have the girl hurt. She's green for all her age and widowhood and has not had much from life. Now, you—you haven't been green since you tweaked your nanny's nose when you were barely two and ten months. I'll wager it's more than noses you're pinching now, and I'll have none of your ways with Mathilda."

"Is there reason I should want to treat Lady Bartone with aught but respect?" Bartone asked archly.

"You're a man, and to most, that's reason enough for anything. I want none of your fine words," snapped Lady Pennypiece. "You've had one taste of my man, Hollon. His manners and looks aren't pretty, but he has many uses, and what he can do to a man is not pretty either."

"The point has been well made, my lady," the viscount said, giving a formal bow. "I have no wish to incur your displeasure, or that of Lady Bartone." He fell silent at the sound of the other's returning footsteps.

Coming back into the room, Mathilda paused, seeing the two politely staring out of the windows. "I am ready, Lord Bartone," she said slowly. "Is everything all right, Aunt Nettie?"

"Of course, my dear," the countess answered. "Now go and watch sharply so you can tell me who has appeared in a new carriage, or what *on dit* the Beau may have to offer," she said lightly, waving her hand in dismissal.

"Are you displeased, Lady Bartone?" the viscount asked as they tooled along a quiet side lane away from the bustle of the busiest London streets.

"No, my lord. Why do you think that?"

"You have not said a word since we left Golden Square."

"I did not think you desired conversation, my lord. You appeared to be preoccupied," Mathilda answered forthrightly. "If there are other matters you have thought needing attention, you could return me to Lady Pennypiece," she offered.

"Surely you have heard that I attend only to women and drink," he laughed challengingly.

"Lord Potters speaks nothing but good of you," she returned quietly.

A strained silence fell over the two as they battled their emotions. Finally Mathilda spoke. "Your horses, Lord Bartone, remind me of a pair in a painting at the Hollows. I believe your father and Sir Bartone are in it also."

"Is there a liver-and-white hunting dog beside them?" he asked.

"Why, I believe there is. Do you know the painting?"

"Yes, my father gave it to Bartone when he was knighted. I can recall his staying at our home here in London during the sessions. Quite an old man he was."

"Yes, but I was very fortunate."

This casual, honest comment drew a new suspicion to Bartone's mind. The smile he threw at Mathilda chilled her, for his eyes were cold and bitter.

"My lord, I thought we were to go to Rotten Row. I do not recognize this area."

"This is a rarely visited part of Hyde Park. I thought you might enjoy a quiet walk without an accompanying audience," Bartone explained, reining his handsome blacks to a halt.

"But Aunt Nettie will expect . . . Is this quite proper, Lord Bartone?" Mathilda asked, glancing about nervously as the viscount stepped down from the phaeton. She could see no one about except the tiger, who was at the team's heads.

"Come, walk with me. Are you afraid?" he laughed mockingly.

His words brought puzzlement to Mathilda's

face and doubt as to the wisdom of going with him, but she accepted the hand he held out.

"Walk the team," Bartone ordered his tiger, keeping hold of Mathilda's hand and pulling her forward as he broke into a light run.

Knowing no one was about, Mathilda raised her skirts with her free hand and followed his lead. The two raced through the sparsely wooded area until Mathilda cried out, "My lord, please, I have lost my shoe."

Bartone swung about instantly, catching her by the waist and swinging her off her feet into his arms.

"My lord," she breathed as he cradled her in his arms.

"Tillie, you are so beautiful," he sighed, as if trying not to speak, a deep tenderness filling his gaze.

Mathilda's spirit leaped to answer his and she leaned forward to accept his kiss. Instead of the gentle caress she expected, he kissed her savagely, and she drew back, startled. His eyes were full of bitterness, even hatred. "Viscount Bartone," Mathilda cried out, bracing both her hands against his chest as he moved to pull her closer again.

Disturbed by her reaction, Bartone eased his grip and slowly set Mathilda on her feet. "Stay here while I find your shoe," he said brusquely.

He returned quickly and knelt to slip the shoe onto her foot.

"Thank you, my lord," she said quietly.

"Do you plan to return to Bartone Hollows soon?" he asked as he rose.

"It is undecided," Mathilda answered. "Lady Pennypiece wishes me to remain until the end of the season, but I am undecided."

"Have you made no plans for your future?"

"I have none, my lord."

"Could you tell me of your childhood?" the viscount asked, after a moment's silence.

Mathilda gave him an incredulous look. His present demeanour and solicitous questions were at strong odds to his rakish behaviour just moments before. "There is nothing of interest in my past, I assure you," she answered cautiously.

"But have you no toy you especially loved? I recall a rocking horse—it had been my father's and his before him; even the reins were tattered. How I loved to ride him, leading soldiers to battle and in parades to celebrate our victories." His features had softened as he reminisced, and Mathilda relaxed.

"I fear there was not much for me. My father was a poor parish cleric, and what little he had he oft gave to others. My mother once made me a doll from a sock, and I suppose that is what was dearest to me then," she said, joining in his mood.

"Was there a special doll you wished to have,

perhaps one you saw in a shop window and always yearned for?" he pursued.

Suspicion returned to Mathilda. Was he trying to learn if she had found the doll? "No, my lord. Perhaps it would be best if we returned to Golden Square now."

He reached out and touched her cheek. "Is that what you wish?"

"I do not understand you, my lord," she said, her frayed emotions threatening to bring on a bout of tears.

"I am attracted to you. Is that so difficult to understand?"

"I do not believe you should be speaking so to me. Please take me home."

"As you wish. We shall speak another time."

The viscount's tone caused a shiver to run through Mathilda. How could a man espouse love and yet be so filled with . . . with hate? she wondered as she gazed at him. He speaks as if to threaten. She could find no answers in his guarded expression, and with a sigh turned back toward the waiting phaeton, a deep sadness welling within her.

Bartone followed, cursing himself, damning Mathilda. He had expected her to fall willingly into his arms, ready to accept whatever he had to offer, as did any courtesan he approached. Her reaction was disconcerting. What he felt for her could be battled only if Pellum could be proven right. Or will even that save you? he asked himself, his heart wincing as he glanced at Mathilda's stress-filled features and knew he was responsible.

CHAPTER SIXTEEN

"You dislike this sudden interest?" Kittridge asked, joining Lord Potters, who was watching Viscount Bartone and Mathilda go through the intricate steps of the minuet in the grand ballroom at Devonshire House.

"Mistrust is more the word," Potters responded. "Will was never cruel as a boy, but since his return from the Indies I have seen behaviour toward women bordering on the savage. I would dislike seeing Lady Mathilda hurt by him."

"She does have a way of making one desire to protect her," Kittridge replied. "Perhaps Bartone feels this way. He was a perfect gentleman this afternoon, according to Hollon."

"I wish I knew what it is that attracts him. He is so changeable. I don't know from one moment to the next what he will do. You don't suppose she cares for him?" Potters asked, turning to Kittridge.

"One should never guess at whom a woman loves," he answered, half frowning, half smiling.

"I rather thought you might be . . . well . . . with Lady Pennypiece approving and all . . ." Potters stumbled verbally.

"The thought has occurred; one could do far worse in a wife."

"Then you do plan to broach the question. I suppose if you love . . ."

"Ah, now, love," Kittridge interrupted him. "That is another matter. Few men are blest with both love and wife in the same woman. Do you care for her?" he asked smoothly.

"No." Potters fidgeted with his spectacles. "A finer sort I've never met. Why, she even reads reports of Parliament and understands them, but . . . He glanced at the couple. "Look. He is taking her out to the gardens. Shouldn't we follow?"

"The viscount is not in his cups this eve—I believe Mathilda will be safe enough," Kittridge assured him. "You worry too much. Come, here is Lady Alice, and she has her delightful cousin with her. I shall introduce you to Miss Teresa. I assure you, her interests do not go beyond her needlework and the rose gardens."

"Rose gardens, you say? I have just added to my own collection with a most fragrant variety of yellow rose." He threw a look at the doors leading to the gardens. "Perhaps they would care to hear of it and have a breath of fresh air."

Kittridge smiled and took Potters's arm. "Don't fret so." He drew him toward the two young ladies. "I am certain Miss Teresa will be only too happy to learn of your addition—to the rose garden, that is."

"The moon is but a crescent this eve," Bartone said, raising a hand to point it out.

"Yes, but see how clearly it shines among the stars," Mathilda answered, lifting her eyes to study it.

"Mathilda—it's much too stern a name for you," Bartone said quietly. "May I call you Tillie?" he asked, capturing her eyes as well as her hands.

"I suppose it will do," she breathed, "for you are . . . family."

"Let us sit and talk. There is an arbour just ahead."

"My lord," Mathilda held back, "would it not be wiser to remain here? Or perhaps we could just walk on the paths?"

Her half-fearful expression made Bartone swear at himself. *She fears a recurrence of this afternoon,* he thought. Forcing light laughter, he placed her hand upon his arm. "Of course, let us walk. And I promise to do nothing which would compromise you, Lady Bartone—if you will forgive my abysmal behaviour earlier in the day," he ended earnestly.

Doubt turned to delight. "It is done, my lord," she said happily.

"'My lord'—must you be so formal? You have said, after all, that I am family. Please call me Will—in private only, if you wish," he added hastily, seeing her hesitation.

"Will is most fitting for you, my lord," Mathilda laughed. "Although at times I am certain 'Willful' may be closer to the mark."

"Ahha, she does have a sharp tongue," he teased. "But what other criticism am I to be given?"

With a glance to see if he was serious in his question, Mathilda said, "It is not my place to find fault, my lord."

"Am I no longer 'Will,' then? Do I have so many offending flaws?" Bartone asked, stepping before Mathilda and raising her face to his with a touch of his hand.

In the darkness of the garden Mathilda could not see his features clearly, but she felt his spirit calling to her own and felt a great need within him clamouring for release. Choosing her words carefully, she spoke slowly, covering his hand with her own as she did. "None of us is without faults. It's recognizing them and working to overcome them as well as we are able that is important. Especially with those faults that harm others as well as ourselves. Many never admit error, seeing only what they wish. If you see faults within yourself, Will, I am certain you can overcome them."

Bartone stood silent, sifting her words as he gazed at her tenderly. Her sincerity was heartening, and for the first time since their breach he thought kindly of Lord Potters.

"I . . . I did not mean to be too personal, my lord," she breathed.

"Will."

"Will," she amended.

"There is no offence taken." He claimed her hand and lowered it, turning so they faced Devonshire House. "I would speak with you longer, but we must return. I would not want to face Lady Pennypiece for causing tongues to wag," he joked lightly.

Mathilda joined in his laughter and glanced up shyly to find him smiling gently at her. "Yes," she replied with exaggerated seriousness as they continued toward the ballroom at a very slow pace, "that would never do."

"A most enjoyable and *profitable* evening," Lady Pennypiece commented to Mathilda as they settled in the coach for the return to Golden Square from Devonshire House. "Did you find the evening to your taste?"

Mathilda leaned back tiredly, but with a smile upon her face. "Yes, but I do wish Lord Potters and Mr. Kittridge would not make *all* their acquaintances dance with me. My feet feel as if I had on slippers that were much too small."

"Dancing does, I suppose, limit the amount of time one can spend in the duchess's beautiful gardens," the countess noted. "But then, at my age, I enjoy them more in the light of day."

Thankful the darkness hid her blush, Mathilda chose not to take the proffered bait.

"I do believe Lord Potters is interested in you, my dear," Lady Pennypiece persisted. "Did he not spend a great deal of time at your side?"

"You know that is only because he is concerned about . . ." she halted. "Aunt Nettie, I am much too tired to fence with you. What is it you wish to know?" Mathilda asked, her tone implying far more than her words.

"I? Wish to know? Why nothing!" Lady Pennypiece answered. "Merely making light conversation to amend for my lack of attention this eve. Lady Potters spoke with some hope of her son's interest in you, is all."

"Ahha! She outdid you, then."

"Young lady, I will thank you to show more respect for your elders. By the way, Kittridge told me you were alone with Bartone more than once this eve."

Despite her effort not to, Mathilda laughed. "Aunt Nettie, no wonder Mr. Brummel approves of you. You are an 'original.' And yes, Viscount

Bartone and I did go for a brief walk in the gardens once or twice."

"It must have proven very beneficial. I notice you speak of him in much more kindly tones than you did earlier in the day." Her voice sharpened suddenly. "Be wary of him, Mathilda."

"He wishes me no harm, Aunt Nettie."

"Has he offered to give you the doll?"

"No, I do not even know if he is aware of the doll or knows of its effects upon me," Mathilda objected.

"You mean you do not wish to know." She paused for a moment. "I learned this afternoon that a man has been questioning the servants about you. It can only mean one thing."

"Lord Bartone would have nothing to do with that."

"He is the only one that has reason to."

"But what of the Pellums?" Mathilda interrupted. "You have said that Mr. Pellum . . ."

"Richard is far too obedient to his mother to do anything on his own initiative, and you must know that his mother feels she knows enough of you already."

"But it makes no sense. He has merely to ask."

"Do you feel you could speak freely of the doll and the stipulation in Howard's will with him?" Lady Pennypiece demanded.

Mathilda could not voice her answer.

"What I say is for your good, Mathilda—to keep you from far greater hurt. Ask yourself. Why should Bartone take this sudden interest in you? Perhaps you are right and he does not know as much about the matter as I think. He may be attempting to learn more. Take care, Mathilda. Do not lose your heart. You may well lose any chance of finding Doll in Red along with it."

CHAPTER SEVENTEEN

A delicate balance was struck between Bartone, Mathilda, and Lady Pennypiece as June came to bloom. For a week after the Devonshire ball, Viscount Bartone appeared wherever Mathilda went, but Lady Pennypiece had decided he was to be held to a short rein. Making the ultimate sacrifice, she refused to go to the cardrooms, instead chaperoning Mathilda as she had never done before, even to the point of accompanying the pair in the viscount's high-perch phaeton. Many young bucks and dandies found themselves adjusting their behaviour under the scrutiny of the countess's upraised quizzing glass and learned a new respct for her wit.

In the third week of June, with the season just past its height, Bartone suddenly and without explanation failed to appear.

"Lord Potters, how good to see you," Mathilda greeted his lordship. "We have missed you."

"My absence has been rather necessary, with

the vote nearing on several issues," he explained. "Had hoped to see Fox here this eve."

"Have you seen Lord Bartone? Is he helping you with these matters?"

"Haven't seen him at Whitehall. Matter of fact, have not seen him anywhere for several days. Do hope he's not gone off on another romp. Must go." He bowed. "I see Fox."

"Of course," Mathilda answered absently as he walked away.

"What did Potters say to bring such a frown to your face?" Kittridge asked, joining her. "Or was the music so very bad?"

"Actually Lady Alice does very well on the harp," Mathilda answered, "but I do wish her mother would not force poor little Lord Francis upon us. He may well be a prodigy, as she hopes, but it will never be with a violin."

"The countess told me you have the headache. Is Lord Francis responsible?" he teased.

Mathilda grinned sheepishly. "I have endured worse, I suppose. But Aunt Nettie was just bursting for a good game of whist and I for a restful evening at home. Do you mind terribly taking me there? It would be fine if you simply called a hackney."

"My coach has already been sent for. I have been wishing to speak with you for some time, and as this will be the first time in weeks you have been permitted from her ladyship's side, I will do well to take advantage of it. Are you ready to go?"

"No, I must take leave of our hostess."

"That has already been done for you, my lady." He bowed formally. "You will find I am always most helpful."

His curious words drew a glance from Mathilda, but she did not speak as he propelled her forward. Reaching the street, he ordered his driver down, instructing the man to wait until his return. Joining her on the seat, he said, "Now we shall have some privacy at last." For the first few minutes his attention was taken with reining the team through the crowded assortment of carriages and coaches about Lord Glashow's residence. Once out of the worst of the snarl, he said, "We have become good friends, have we not, Mathilda?"

She nodded, a sinking feeling in the pit of her stomach at so strange a beginning to the conversation.

"We enjoy each other's company—seem suited, in other words," Kittridge continued. "Do you not agree?"

"I . . . well, of course I find your company very pleasant. You have been very kind and . . ."

"And," he interrupted, "and you are a widow—alone in this world. Oh, deuce all," he laughed at himself. "I am making a mess of this business. Come, Mathilda, say you will marry me."

Faced with what she had feared he was broaching, she answered, "I cannot, Kitt. You mean well,

I know, and I do care for you, but . . . it . . . it would not be fair to you, for it is not love I feel for you."

"Love would come in time," he returned. "Many marriages have less in the beginning than we would have."

"You cannot have thought this out, Kitt. Why, I have not even been introduced to your family. Surely they expect you to marry well. I have nothing. Even the clothes I wear have been purchased by the countess," Mathilda protested.

"That is not the true reason, is it?" he asked, a rueful smile upon his lips.

"No," she answered slowly, reaching out and touching his arm, "but I do thank you."

"If ever you change your mind, you have only to let me know."

"I could not hold you to such unwise words, for you would regret it bitterly when you met the one whom you could truly love. I married once for security. I could not do it again."

Both fell silent, wrapped in separate thoughts. As they neared No. 31 Golden Square, Kittridge spoke again. "Let us remain as friends and not let this linger uncomfortably. Of course, we shall say nothing of it to the countess."

"I will gladly agree to that," Mathilda replied with relief. "And I do appreciate your offer."

Kittridge smiled and nodded. No further mention was made of what had passed, and the two slipped into their usual conversation, but Mathilda would not have forgotten the matter so quickly had she seen the concern with which Kittridge watched her enter the house or the frown which he carried back to Glashow's.

"Good morn, Aunt Nettie," Mathilda said, entering the breakfast room early the next morn. "You look unusually well pleased with yourself this morn. May I presume you had a winning night?"

"Fair, rather fair," Lady Pennypiece responded in measured tones. "A most interesting eve. I almost woke you when I returned."

"Oh"—Mathilda raised her eyes from her plate—"what has happened? What did you hear?" she asked cautiously.

"I saw an old cousin whom I had almost forgotten existed."

Relaxing, since the news did not concern either Kittridge or Bartone, Mathilda sipped her tea. "Did she lose a large amount to you?"

"She? Oh, my cousin. No, it is he—Sir Grewould, and no, he did not lose. Honestly, Mathilda, you speak as if I live only to fleece others. Well, let us forget that." Lady Pennypiece leaned forward, pointing a bony finger. "Sir Grewould should interest you, young lady. He made me recall my youth, and"—she dragged out the word—"he mentioned a most curious fact."

"What? That your wig was slightly askew?" teased Mathilda.

"Mind your manners, miss. I think it is time you were removed from this corrupting city for a time," Lady Pennypiece quipped, with feigned anger.

The saucy smile upon Mathilda's lips trembled and was gone. "If you wish, Aunt Nettie. I can be ready this afternoon," she said, keeping her eyes fast upon her food.

"That will not be necessary—two days hence—this weekend you may note—will do. I am glad you agree to go. A rest from our hectic pace will do us both good, and you may at last be successful," she ended triumphantly.

"But I don't understand," Mathilda stammered, totally bewildered by the other's words.

"Of course not, my dear," the countess returned haughtily, "and my wig is never crooked *unless* I decide it should be so. Style, you know." She patted the elaborate array of powdered curls.

"Forgive me, please," Mathilda said, a smile belying her contrite tones.

"Did you believe for a moment that I would send you away?" Lady Pennypiece asked, becoming quite serious. "After all my conspiring to keep you here? Do you not know what your coming has meant to me?" she asked, her voice breaking on the last word.

"Aunt Nettie," Mathilda said, startled by the

sudden crack in the old woman's seemingly impervious skin. Tears came as she reached across to take her hand.

"There you go—tears," scolded Lady Pennypiece, raising her napkin to dab at her own. "Will the young never learn." A loud sniff and a scornful shake of the head indicated the depth of her feelings. "I arrange a simple weekend in the country and we sit here acting as if a death notice has just arrived. Enough."

"Oh, Aunt Nettie." Mathilda rose and hugged the old woman. "What was that most curious fact your cousin mentioned?" she asked, "and where are we going for the weekend?"

"You still doubt your interest in this, eh?" Lady Pennypiece teased. "I have not been idle. My servants have returned from Pennywise and . . ."

"When? Why was I not told? What did they find? Are we to go to Pennywise?" Mathilda asked excitedly.

"Calm yourself, my dear. Excitement is bad for the complexion." She sighed at Mathilda's eagerness. "I did not mean to make you think the doll had been found. But there is still hope it will be," she hurried on. "That is what I meant by Sir Grewould. We are to go to his country estate."

With her last, meagre hope evaporated, Mathilda returned to her chair dejectedly. "There is no need for a weekend in the country, Aunt Nettie. I have spent my entire life there."

"But we go for a specific reason. You see, Sir Grewould mentioned his late wife's habit of collecting gewgaws."

"How can that aid me?"

"Many years ago her passion was for dolls, and I know I gave her several. She and I were friends but lost contact as she settled to raising a family. But the important thing is that the collections are still in the house on the estate. This weekend we shall discover if Doll in Red is there."

CHAPTER EIGHTEEN

"Welcome home, my lord," Green greeted the viscount, noting his master's healthy glow. "Your journey was pleasant?"

"Very," Bartone answered. "Is Lynn about?"

"Yes, my lord, he is in his office now. But Mr. Nettles has returned. This is the third day he has awaited your return."

"Send him to my office and tell Lynn I want to see him as soon as I have finished with Nettles. Also see that my landau is readied," Bartone ordered, striding to his office.

"My lord," Mr. Nettles greeted the viscount as he entered.

Bartone tossed aside the letters he had been going through. "What did you learn?"

"Actual facts, my lord, were easily obtained." He handed an envelope to the viscount. "This contains all dates—the lady's birth, marriage date, Sir Bartone's death. It also has a report on what I learned."

"Is there anything you have to add to what you have written?"

"Facts, my lord, don't always tell all there is to know," Nettles began. "Often one needs to go beyond them."

"What is it you are trying to tell me?" Bartone asked, his patience thinning.

"Lady Bartone is not well thought of by many people of standing in Horley. Nor did Squire Pellum and his wife have a kind word for her. To believe these is to have the lady a tart of the worst sort." He watched as Bartone tensed, his fists clenching. "But there are others that tell a different tale, speaking of kindness and generosity on her part," Nettles ended.

"What others do you mean?" Bartone demanded coldly.

"Mostly the poor, honest folk who have been helped by her ladyship. Even before she married Sir Bartone, the lady was known to be willing to help in any way she could, even though she and her mother were as poor as most, or poorer. Some took her marriage as just dues, well deserved on her part. She's been much the same with them since, still giving of herself . . ."

"And Bartone's money," the viscount finished for him.

Nettles shook his head. "If I were you, my lord, I'd believe the poor folk," he assured him.

"Did her servants support these poor folk?"

Brushing back his hair, Nettles screwed his face up in uncertainty. "About them, my lord, well, it seems there are only three—four if you count a halfwit by the name of Sal."

"Three. Has she left off many since she came to London?"

"No, my lord, that's all Sir Bartone had when he wed her, and those three are almost of his age. Some claim the servants disliked the marriage as much as Mrs. Pellum, but I've my doubts. The little I learned from them seems to say they think of the young lady more as a daughter than a mistress. And they are worried about her. They seem to be concealing something. What, I could not learn—very close to the mouth they were, my lord, very close."

"That will be all, Nettles. I doubt I'll have further need of your services." Bartone wrote briefly on a piece of paper and handed it to the little man. "Will that be sufficient for expenses and your fee?" he asked.

"If ever you have need, just send word, my lord," Nettles responded, raising his eyes from the figure, which surpassed his fee by several quid.

"Green will direct you to my secretary's office. Give him that and he will take care of you."

"Good day, my lord. Pleased to have served you, and don't worry none 'bout the lady. She's a good sort." The viscount's instant scowl sent him scurrying from the room.

The man gone, Bartone opened the envelope and withdrew the material. Nettles's neat, precise handwriting detailed all he had said. As Bartone read along, his brow grew darker and darker. "Rot," he exclaimed, tossing the papers down when he had finished. Experience in the West Indies, where rivalries among the few privileged, upper-class women were often ferocious, should have taught him what jealousy could do, but he was blind to it.

"Tillie," he moaned aloud, glancing at the papers. *Her life should deny all you are thinking*, his heart told his mind. *But why were the servants worried? Had she threatened them? Wouldn't Sir Bartone have taken care of them? But wait—what if they had not been taken care of? Then she could control all.* Question after question raced through his mind. All ended at one point. No matter where he began, he ended with the mystery of Doll in Red.

"You wished to see me, my lord?" Lynn asked, entering the office after a polite knock.

"Be seated, Lynn," Bartone said, taking his own chair. "How long has it been since funds were released to do the necessary repairs on the cottages at Bartone Hall?"

"The last time funds were given was six months before your father died, my lord," Lynn answered.

"Why has none been released since? Those cottages have leaking roofs, broken windows—if windows at all," Bartone noted angrily.

An uneasy look came to Lynn's face. His task as secretary to an absentee landlord had been difficult. The viscount's return had done nothing to ease matters, as he had refused until lately to take any interest. "My lord, I wrote to you oft of these matters, and many others in the past," he explained carefully. "Since I received no reply, my authority was limited. There is much I could not do."

"I want you to begin compiling lists of all the necessary improvements, as well as other recommendations you may have. Order whatever is of immediate necessity for my people's welfare. Consult my agent, Atler, on the matter. After we review matters, you shall see to what extent my presence is required. Learn Atler's demands and return to me." Bartone rose. "I regret I cannot go with you, but for the present my time shall be given to the government. I mean to assume my seat in the Lords."

Rising when his lordship did, Lynn now bowed. "May I welcome you home at last, my lord. It is very good to have you."

Bartone stepped around his desk and walked with the secretary to the door. "It is my hope that with your help the neglect caused by my absence can be remedied."

"It will take time, my lord," Lynn cautioned, "and much attention on your part."

"Then let us begin," the viscount urged. "See to the matters at once."

"Why so dour an expression?" Green asked Lynn as they met in the corridor outside Bartone's office. "The change in his lordship should please you."

"It is a hopeful sign," Lynn said slowly.

"Hopeful? Now, what is in that head of yours?"

"His lordship has been rather volatile of late, Mr. Green. One can only hope his interest is not a passing fancy." Having voiced his concern aloud, Lynn nodded and walked on.

For a few moments Green watched him, pondering the truth of his words. Then, recalling the summons of the bell, he strode hurriedly to his master.

"My hat and gloves," Bartone commanded as Green entered. "I do not believe I shall return before early evening, but I shall come to change for the opera."

"Very good, my lord."

At the door he took his hat and gloves and asked, "Has Baron Potters called at any time during my absence?"

"No, my lord," the butler answered, opening the door.

In a few quick strides Bartone was at the landau's side. Springing in, he ordered the driver to Whitehall.

The hoots of those in the galleries and the mumble of voices below interfered with the present speaker's words but did not come as a surprise to Bartone as he took the seat pointed out to him. A few acquaintances nodded coolly, but most were plotting with their neighbours. A very few listened to Charles Fox's eloquent testimonial for the abolition of the slave trade. For some time Bartone listened and observed. His ignorance became appallingly evident to him as the hours passed, and when he decided to leave, it was with the determination to learn much more of the issues being debated. *Tillie has made me realize so much*, he thought as he rose to leave. A deep frown came to him—his heart said to love her; his mind warned against it.

So preoccupied had he become that he collided squarely with another gentleman in the outer chambers. "Pardon me," the viscount began, then broke into a smile. "By Napoleon's bootstraps, if it isn't just the chap I wished to see," he exclaimed.

Lord Potters eyed Bartone apprehensively.

"Surprised to see me, are you?" Bartone asked with a wry smile. "But I am keeping you. Had you planned to stay till the end of the debate?"

"Why, no. I have some papers to give Fox and

one or two others. The debate is in the primary stages yet," Potters answered cautiously. "Why?"

"Could you come with me, then—when you've finished?"

"I suppose I could. Yes, I could if it is important to you."

"It is very important. I shall wait for you here—friend?" Bartone said.

Smiling openly, Potters nodded.

"I've been forced to do a lot of thinking of late," Bartone spoke, breaking the awkward silence that had hung over the pair since the beginning of the drive. "When one is in the country there is little else to do."

"Where have you been? I didn't realize until Lady Mathilda asked about you that I hadn't seen you about," Lord Potters commented.

"Potts, I've been to Bartone Hall, and my eyes were opened to its dismal state. I deserved every word you ever gave me on my ways—and many you didn't. I am not good at apologies, but . . ."

A hand touched his. "Will, it need not be said. We are *old* friends. I'm glad to see you are more settled, that you mean to take your seat."

"They have little use for me. I know it is with good reason, but I mean to change that. Potts, there is so much I do not know, so much with which I am unfamiliar."

"I can help you there, and so will many others. You were always quick to learn, Will."

"Thank God for friends such as you, Potts. I knew you would be as dependable as you've always been."

Both men relaxed.

"Why did you go to the Hall?" Lord Potters asked, his curiosity tweaking him.

"Someone said something about changing things about yourself that harm others. Well, I decided to go to those who are most dependent upon me, those whose existence I had forgotten for a long time, if the truth be known."

"And here I thought you'd gone . . ."

"Careening across the countryside, endangering the local citizenry?" Bartone finished for him, then grinned sheepishly. "What a shock it was to see what my neglect had done. I'm sending Lynn there to begin work. There is so much to be done. What a fool I've been," he ended.

"I knew you'd come aright in the end, Will," Potters said. "It's good to have you back."

"And good to be back. I had almost forgotten what fresh air and sunlight could do for the soul."

Silence fell as the two men ruminated upon the past.

"What is it, Will?" Potters asked as he saw Bartone stiffen.

"Nothing," the viscount answered, giving a curt

nod to Kittridge, whose carriage they met and passed. "Do you plan to go to the opera tonight?"

"I suppose I shall. But there is no reason for you to go," Potters noted in answer.

"What is your meaning?"

"Lady Pennypiece and her guest are remaining home, since they have to prepare for a weekend outing in the country," he answered with feigned disinterest.

"They go to Pennywise? Or to the Hollows?"

"For one planning on catching up with two years of indifference, you seem unusually interested in your aged cousin's activities. And I had not thought you overly fond of her."

Bartone scowled. "It is her butler I do not care for. Far more true to say she is not fond of me. Do you know their direction?"

"You deserve to be fobbed off, but"—his friend broke into a wide grin—"I shall have mercy on you. They go to Sir Grewould's estate. He is a cousin of Lady Pennypiece's, I gather."

"Why would they be going there?" Bartone wondered aloud.

"Some nonsense about needing a rest before the last rigours of the season," the Baron answered.

"Does Kittridge go with them?"

"I believe not. He seems preoccupied these days. Asked about you, he did. Wouldn't be surprised if he tried to make a match with Lady Mathilda," he added, watching Bartone closely.

The other's eyes narrowed. "Do you think she'd accept him?" he asked quietly.

"Don't know. Rather likes him, I gather. He's from the best of families—money aplenty. What more could she want?" Potters said lightly, not realizing the damage he was doing. "A great improvement on old Bartone, it would be."

"Was there any other mention of why they were going to Grewould's?" Bartone asked after a few minutes' thought.

Something in the viscount's voice struck an odd note with Potters. He shook off the feeling and answered, "His wife had a habit of collecting things. Seems Lady Pennypiece wanted to see the assortments. A doll collection—that was it. Said she'd given several dolls to Lady Grewould and wanted to see them again." He glanced at Bartone, but the other was far away in thought. *He's troubled by something, something more than Lady Mathilda being out of reach for a few days,* Potters told himself. Will the change last? Can he throw off whatever has been eating at him, or does it still hold to him like a leech?

Bartone was no longer thinking about his own rehabilitation. Instead his thoughts leaped from Grewould and Doll in Red to the more pressing question of Kittridge and Mathilda.

CHAPTER NINETEEN

"What is it, Mathilda? You have not glanced beyond your gloves since we began this journey. Does the countryside displease you?" Lady Pennypiece asked as the coach carried them toward Grewould's acres.

"Did you say something, Aunt Nettie?" Mathilda asked, taking her eyes from her lap.

"Now, see, you have not heard a word I've said for the past two days. What is so heavy in your thoughts?"

"The doll, I suppose. It seems such a long journey for such little hope," Mathilda said, clasping and unclasping her hands nervously.

"There is more to it than that. Ah, I know—that letter from your butler . . ."

"His name is Dannon."

"Dannon, then. You have been upset ever since you received it. What was in it?" Lady Pennypiece demanded.

"There was nothing." Mathilda paused, a worried frown creasing her smooth forehead. "Dannon said a man had been to Horley. He asked many questions about me."

"Was that all?"

"But many do not think well of me there."

"Are you concerned that someone was asking questions, or about the answers that were being given?"

"Oh, I don't know. Everything is so confusing now. I don't know what I think about anything." Mathilda threw a beseeching look at the countess.

"There is little I can do, my dear," she answered the look. "You are tired from all the activity of late and preparing for the journey."

"Couldn't we turn back?" Mathilda asked. "I feel as if I ought not to be going, as if something were happening and I could stop it . . ."

"What is happening—where? Mathilda, you're letting your mind run away with your feelings. Now we are almost there. A good night's rest in this invigorating, country air will raise your spirits." She patted Mathilda's knee. "You shall see. They will soar with the sunrise."

The words were no comfort to Mathilda. She looked out of the coach's window and saw only the gloom of an incoming storm. Bartone's face was reflecting in it, and here too, it seemed, he was taunting, challenging. Had Will sent the man to Horley? Why did he disappear without a word? Her heart ached for the answers. Oh, that I had never come to London, she thought, overcome by a dour foreboding, which loomed ever stronger, as did the gathering clouds.

Lady Pennypiece, who had been watching Mathilda carefully, noted, "It does look like a bit of rain, doesn't it? But we are almost there, I believe." She leaned forward and peered out of the coach's window. "There is the house, just a short distance now. Do not let Sir John alarm you if his greeting is not too warm," she cautioned Mathilda.

For an instant Mathilda thought she saw fear on Lady Pennypiece's face, but accustomed to her eccentricities, she paid little heed, shifting her attention instead to the large house looming before them.

Of Cotswold stone, the building peered at them with its three stories of leaded, curtained windows like many half-closed eyes. Noble despite time's ravages, the house was covered with ivy and moss and blended in with the green of the park surrounding it.

No one came to greet the women as they descended from the coach. "Isn't it odd, Aunt Nettie?" Mathilda commented as she glanced about and saw no one, not even a gardener.

"Sir John may not have expected us to arrive so early. Many sleep late after traveling, but I never could abide an inn longer than necessary. Let us go in."

"Wait until someone collects our baggage and

directs you to the stables," the countess ordered her coachmen. "Let us not dawdle. It could begin raining any moment from the look of the weather," she told Mathilda, leading the way up the flagstone walk to the main doors. The porticoed entrance showed signs of fitful care, as did the lawns and gardens.

The clatter of hooves upon the drive halted the objection Mathilda was about to make as Lady Pennypiece reached to open the doors unbidden. Both turned to see who came.

A pudgy man atop a huge black hunter galloped across the ill-manicured lawn, halting at the portico's edge. The servants, following on poorer beasts, halted at the drive's edge; one dismounted and came running to take Sir John's horse as he dismounted.

"Netta, what brings you to my door?" he asked, stamping forward, his reddened face showing the effect of a hard ride and ample spirits.

"Now, Sir John, you know you invited me to spend some time with you," Lady Pennypiece admonished him, raising her quizzing glass.

"Rather odd"—he removed his hat and scratched his balding head—"that I recall nothing of it. Haven't had many callers since Elizabeth popped off, 'cept the children, and I ignore them."

"Then we are just what you need. Won't you

see our baggage and coach taken care of? I am exhausted," she sighed.

"Little for your comfort here," Sir John grunted. "Few servants and all."

"I bring my own," the countess cut him. "You have not met Howard's wife." She took Mathilda's arm. "Lady Mathilda, our cousin, Sir John Grewould."

"Pleased, ma'am," Sir John grunted again, still hesitating to invite them in.

"I feel faint," Lady Pennypiece breathed, leaning toward Mathilda.

"See to them, see to them," Grewould sharply ordered the groom who held his hunter. "Get the abigail from the coach top. Hurry! Supper best be ready, after this day," he harrumphed to himself. "Dine early we do, at a proper time," Sir John continued, gazing distastefully at the two women. "Was in the army, you know," he said to no one in particular as they entered the house, Lady Pennypiece suddenly feeling much improved. "I like things done in the proper way at the proper time."

The first few drops of rain splattered onto the flagstones as Mathilda glanced back, a fitting portent for the day to come.

The rain was falling in a steady rhythm when Mathilda awoke the next morn. A chill belied the June day, and the gloom of the heavy clouds filled the room. Drawing the coverlet closer about her, she surveyed her quarters. The room's heavy furniture, drab curtains, and dusty ledges were a strong reminder of the Hollows. She thought of Dannon and Mrs. Bertie and shivered. It must be your imagination, she told herself, to think it cold. Rising, she dressed hastily, choosing the heaviest gown she had brought.

Sir Grewould must have conjured up this weather, she murmured aloud, thinking of his cold reception and how he had ignored them last eve. With her toilet complete, she wondered what to do. Few sounds had come from the large house, and she did not know if Sir John or the servants were about. If had been quite clear that Lady Pennypiece had descended upon Sir John without warning. A knock at the door caused Mathilda to start. "Yes?" she called out.

"Lady Pennypiece requests that you come to breakfast, my lady," sounded a voice Mathilda recognized as the maid who had helped unpack.

Opening the door, Mathilda asked, "Her ladyship is to breakfast already?"

"And Sir Grewould also," the girl answered. "Very punctual is his lordship. I'll show you the way if you wish."

"Please do." Mathilda smiled her gratitude.

"Good morn," Lady Pennypiece greeted Mathilda cheerfully as she entered the breakfast room. "I was just telling Sir John how well you slept in the country air."

"The room is very comfortable," Mathilda told her host, who continued eating as if she had never spoken.

Lady Pennypiece motioned for her to sit and remain silent. "Sir John," she spoke loudly, "since the rain prevents our touring your gardens, would you consider showing us through the house? It has been many years since I stayed with you. I would love to see some of Elizabeth's collections, especially the dolls."

"Collections . . . Hurumph. Nasty things—they only collect dust, you know. Nasty." He returned to his eating with vigour.

A shrug and eye-rolling look from Lady Pennypiece told Mathilda her opinion of their cousin. Setting her teacup firmly in its saucer after draining it, the countess tried once more. "Many years ago . . ." She paused. "Sir John? Sir John?" she shouted.

He looked up from his eating. "What's that?"

"I was saying," Lady Pennypiece continued, "many years ago I gave Elizabeth some dolls for her collection. Would you consider letting me take any of those I had given her as a remembrance of our friendship? It would please me so."

Sir John stared for a moment, then returned to his food without a word.

Rising, Lady Pennypiece signaled for Mathilda to follow her from the room.

"How long have you been up, Aunt Nettie?"

she asked, once they were in the corridor. "I never heard a sound."

"That is because our rooms are in a part of the house never used these days," she answered. "Come, let us begin."

"Begin? You don't mean to look for the doll collection, do you?" Mathilda asked, suspicious of the gleam in the other's eyes.

"Of course not," she replied gaily. "You are going to assist me."

"We dare not. What would Sir John say?"

"He'll probably never rise from his table," Lady Pennypiece poohed. "If we can judge by yester-eve, we can be certain of no interruption."

"But the servants?"

"They will not dare to approach me. My looks and manners do have some benefits, you see," she winked. "Now, I believe Elizabeth kept some of her collections in one of the salons on this floor. Come along," she said sweeping forward majestically.

Mathilda's fear was overcome by curiosity as they progressed from room to room. Each chamber revealed another interest of the late Lady Elizabeth. Buttons, hats, vases, vinaigrettes, fans, quizzing glasses, and music boxes were only a few of the dust-covered wonders they discovered.

"Where have you been?" Sir John scolded when they came from the fourth room on their expedition. "Thought you wanted to see Elizabeth's dolls."

"We do," Lady Pennypiece assured him, taking his arm. "Could we now? I do believe we are not occupied at the moment." She looked at Mathilda and winked.

"Then to it," Sir John urged. "A cold collation will be served soon."

Giving her wig a jaunty push, Lady Pennypiece stepped out with Sir John. Mathilda followed, fearful of bursting into laughter at the picture the odd pair presented.

His lordship led them past the rooms they had searched and on toward a pair of large doors, which opened with a mighty creak after being threatened by his pudgy hands. Inside, glass doors encased shelves of books. One end of the room was engulfed by a huge stone fireplace while at the opposite end stood glass cases filled with dolls. Tiny miniatures of wood, clay, and bisque reposed on the center shelves, their dainty dresses and suits, mere swatches of lace and silk, correct to the most minuscule detail. Their arrangement led the eye naturally on to the slightly larger dolls, with their opaque brown glass eyes and flaxen hair. Intermingled were dolls made with more advanced skill—some with human hair.

The women's gazes traveled smoothly, admiringly, over the multitude of richly costumed dolls, halting here and there to take in an especially intricate dress or highly colourful costume. French fashion dolls, or "fashion babies," as the French noblewomen called them, had been used to keep abreast of fashion trends during the fourteenth, fifteenth, and sixteenth centuries. They delighted the eye with their delicate period toilets. Over row after row Mathilda and Lady Pennypiece scanned the dolls, marveling while searching, but unaware of the irony of all the eyes staring back emptily.

"I never quite realized Elizabeth had so many," Lady Pennypiece noted, walking slowly toward the cases.

"She liked them best," Sir John said proudly. "They're the only ones that don't collect dust."

"How many are there?" Mathilda asked, staring in wonder.

"Never counted," he returned. Waving at the collection, he concluded, "Enough."

All eyes went back to the amazing array. There were dolls in court dress, in evening wear, and in day gowns. Some were dressed as peasants and servants.

Both women studied them, row after row, shelf upon shelf. Their hopeful expectations slowly melted from their faces.

Among all of these dolls there were only ten dressed in red, and none was Doll in Red.

CHAPTER TWENTY

Melancholy brought on by the failure to find Doll in Red, the dreary rain, and an unwilling host prompted Lady Pennypiece to order her coach readied and the baggage packed. Far from objecting to so precipitate a departure, Sir John welcomed it with relief. He saw them off in the rain, which had lightened, and returned to his table to partake of a proper dinner.

In the coach Mathilda stared out of the window. All was going awry, and each lurch closer to London increased her apprehension.

Safely back at No. 31 Golden Square, Mathilda found nothing to dispel her foreboding. Viscount Bartone avoided her, or worse, stood in the distance staring. Lady Pennypiece launched her upon a new round of balls and soirees. Kittridge escorted them to the theatre and the opera; he took Mathilda shopping and even on a visit to Tunbridge Wells. But all failed to raise her spirits beyond a weak smile. Even Lord Potters noticed her melancholia and sought to cheer her with reports of Bartone's help with the bill against the slave trade. But even he wondered at his friend's sudden coldness toward Mathilda.

Realizing that they were all troubled for her, she assumed a false gaiety, which relieved them all save Lady Pennypiece, who saw through the pose. The countess also noticed that Mathilda had become restless, as if constantly looking for someone, whenever they were out. Only the appearance of Bartone quieted this agitation, she learned, and it was also evident that the viscount, though seemingly reformed and now highly spoken of by many, went out of his way to snub them.

"Where have you been?" Lord Potters protested as Viscount Bartone ran up to him in the outer chamber of the Lords. "They are about to put it to the vote."

"Matters on the reform issue," Bartone panted. "Let us go in now."

"You go in. I must see if I can find Clarke and Mahew. They wandered out during Grenville's speech."

"Then let me help you look for them. Wait, here they are."

Together the four men entered just in time to take part in the vote. Leaving some time later, they went to Brooks's. It was evening when Bartone and Potters returned to the viscount's home.

"What will you do now, Potts?" Bartone asked, pouring brandy for them both.

"There is the last vote on the reform bill to be taken on the morrow. I suppose after that I shall go to the country for the summer and prepare for the fall session."

"Do you suppose Wilberforce will drop his efforts after today's failure?"

"No, he has seen years of failure. What is important is that his effort gains support each year. In a year, perhaps two, he will manage to get a bill through the Commons and then we will have a greater chance in the Lords," Potters replied.

"We? I don't know about myself. All this work—you have been at it constantly for weeks and all the while knowing you would fail? Why do it?"

"Because it matters. The day will come when men of any colour will no longer be shipped like cattle across the seas. How can life have meaning if we run each time we fail?"

Bartone moved to refill Potters's glass.

"No, Will, I've enough. And so have you," he noted, watching the viscount refill his own. "We will need you on the morrow."

Gulping the brandy, Bartone sat down. "I don't know, Potts. I'm tired. So tired."

"You've a right to be, with all you've tried to

do. How is Lynn doing at the Hall?" he asked, trying to change Bartone's tread of thought.

"Troubles. Nothing but troubles. Each new repair reveals more that needs attending. The people are clamouring for more and more."

"Neglect is seldom righted in a week or a month, Will. You knew what you faced."

"Don't lecture, Potts. Not now. You'd better go. I'm bad company this eve."

"Why don't you come with me? I mean to stop in at Mahew's ball," Potters urged his friend.

Bartone shook his head. "I'll think on it. Perhaps later I'll come by." After seeing Potters to the door, he returned to his office and poured another brandy. The pace he had been keeping for the last weeks was collecting its dues. Exhaustion triggered depression, which grew deeper and deeper as he drank.

Falling asleep, Bartone dreamed of the Indies and awoke filled with an anger he had sought to leave behind. He rose, quaffed a drink, and paced to and fro. *What had Potts mentioned? Mahew's ball. There is diversion for me there,* he thought, and ordered his phaeton.

"Thank you, Lord Potters," Mathilda told the baron, accepting the lemonade he had brought her. "There is such a crush this eve."

"This is one of the last balls of the season," he replied. "Everyone wishes to make a last appearance before departing for the summer. Will you be going to Pennywise with Lady Pennypiece?"

"No, I mean to return to the Hollows, perhaps next week," she answered. "I have imposed upon the countess too long already."

"She has never been in higher spirits. My mother says you have done her a goodly turn by staying," he assured her.

"It is my dance, Mathilda," Kittridge said, joining them. "Sorry about the vote today, Potters."

"It was expected. There will be another day."

Kittridge nodded. "But now is the time to forget serious matters, my lady." He bowed, holding out his hand.

Mathilda placed her hand in his with a smile. "I regard my steps very seriously, and so would you if I did not," she warned.

Bidding Potters to find a partner, they joined the dancers for the country set. By its end, perspiration was beaded upon Mathilda's brow, and Kittridge led her to the gardens. "It is a very warm evening," he commented, "but at least we have a breeze here."

"Thank goodness for these light muslin gowns," Mathilda returned, dabbing at her face. "I am surprised you gentlemen survive once the weather warms." She fanned herself with her kerchief.

"Ah, a woman of compassion at last," he laughed lightly, taking her hand. "You must let me return it," he said, becoming serious. "Could you not tell me what is worrying you?"

"I worried? You are mistaken . . ."

"No, I am not. But I will not press you." He kissed her hand lightly.

Impulsively, she kissed his cheek. "Thank you, Kitt." Shaking her head at the question she saw upon his face, she said, "I have not changed my mind. This week will be my last here. Now off with you before some poor damsel dissolves in tears because you have not claimed your dance with her. I will sit here for a time. This dance has not been spoken for."

With a sigh, Mathilda settled back, wiggling her toes in her satin slippers. One slipped from her heel as she did so and she raised her skirt to reach it. Bending over to redo the slipper's ties, she found the light blocked by a man's figure. "I am fine, Kitt. It is only my . . ." Her voice trailed off as she raised her eyes and confronted Bartone's angry stance.

"So it is Kitt now," he swore. "You are to marry him, then."

"Mr. Kittridge has been very kind to me, Lord Bartone," she replied, shrinking from his glare, "but I am not to wed him."

"He has not asked?"

"What Mr. Kittridge does or does not do is of no concern of yours," she retorted, trying to draw strength from her growing anger.

Bartone grabbed her arm and pulled her upright. "Has he asked?"

"Yes, my lord, and I have refused," Mathilda answered with tears threatening as she looked into Bartone's eyes.

"Refused—but why? Wasn't he wealthy enough for you?" he sneered.

"I don't know what you mean," she returned, a tear finding its way down her cheek. "I know nothing of Mr. Kittridge's affairs."

"Why do you persist in this studied ignorance of his title? An odd way to treat one of the gentry when you insist upon being 'my lady.'"

Wincing as his grip tightened on her arm, Mathilda retorted, "How can you object to a man's name? Release me. You have no right . . ."

"You want me to think you really believe he is *Mister* Kittridge," Bartone said, incredulous. "You really do, don't you? Is that why you refused his offer?"

"Why would I refuse a man because of his name? Are you mad?" Mathilda asked, beginning to fear it must be so.

Bartone released his hold. "So you wanted a title. Was Potters to be your choice, then? You will find he is not fool enough. No, you lost your chance, my lady," he mocked her. "You could have been Lord Kittridge Pennypiece's wife. Now you shall be no one's." A bitter laugh taunted her confusion. "Oh, yes, he is Lord Pennypiece. Ask anyone—your precious countess. Kittridge is a given name."

Numbly shaking her head, Mathilda walked away. Tears no longer came—she was beyond them.

CHAPTER TWENTY-ONE

For most of the night Mathilda lay awake in the darkness of her room. She had taken a hackney cab to Golden Square and feigned sleep when Lady Pennypiece looked in on her. Daylight had not eased her aching heart. Dressing was a mechanical chore done from habit as she tried to sort out her thoughts.

"Mathilda, I am glad to see you up," Lady Pennypiece said, entering her room. "Were you taken ill? Why, you are frightfully pale," she exclaimed. "Let me send for a doctor."

"Is Kitt your son?" Mathilda blurted, unable to contain the question any longer.

"So you have found it out," Lady Pennypiece sighed. "Is that why you left so suddenly last eve?"

"Why . . . why did you lie?" Mathilda asked, fighting back tears.

"It was harmless, or meant to be; an accident that was compounded. Remember when you first met Kittridge in the lane outside of Farnham? He said his name was Kittridge—am I not correct?"

Swallowing hard, Mathilda nodded.

"Was it not you, yourself, who presumed to address him as *Mister* Kittridge?" Lady Pennypiece put her arms around Mathilda. "How was he to know he would see you again? It seemed senseless for him to explain. Then, later, he did not want to embarrass you, and he could not see the harm, there was no other reason."

Her head on the old woman's shoulder, Mathilda broke into sobs. Lady Pennypiece held her until they ceased, then handed her a kerchief. "Who told you?" she asked.

"Viscount Bartone," Mathilda said through sniffles. "He . . ." Tears came again.

Her lips in a thin line, Lady Pennypiece patted Mathilda's shoulder.

"I want to go home today," Mathilda said, raising her tear-reddened face.

"There is something we must do before you go," the countess said quietly. "I was going to suggest it soon, and I think today will be the day."

"The day for what?" Mathilda asked, wiping her eyes.

"Ever since our return from Grewould I have searched every corner of my memory for what I could have done with Doll in Red."

"Oh, forget her, Aunt Nettie. I should never have come," she protested.

"I thought you were concerned with the welfare of Bannon . . ."

"You mean Dannon," Mathilda corrected, sniffling.

"Dannon, then, and his wife. Do you no longer care what happens to them?"

"Of course I do. Their fate is like a puppy—you can't help but trip over it wherever you turn."

"Then you must do everything necessary to find Doll in Red."

"But we have."

"No. I recalled earlier this morn that I gave the doll to a niece of Viscount Bartone's—the fourth viscount—many years ago."

"Aunt Nettie, you thought you gave it to Lady Grewould. You do not know, cannot remember. It was just too long ago," Mathilda disagreed tiredly.

"I recall this quite clearly," the old woman said with stubborn pride. "The niece lived with them before the present viscount was born. And she died shortly after his birth. A riding accident, I believe. Never mind that, though. I remember that Lady Bartone told me the doll and some other toys had been put aside in the nursery to await the coming of a daughter. However, the present viscount was to be their only child."

"Then he has the doll and it is out of our reach," Mathilda said, totally defeated.

"But he may not know it is there. Don't you

see?" Lady Pennypiece explained patiently. "Why would he think to look in the nursery?"

"Even if he hasn't, what can we do? Oh, no," she waved her hands in protest, seeing that gleam in Lady Pennypiece's eyes. "I will not do it."

"There will be so little involved," the countess shrugged innocently. "You cannot hesitate."

"The chances of the doll's being there are very slim—in fact it is impossible," Mathilda continued to object. "If the doll was not at Pennywise, nor Grewould, why should it be in the viscount's house?"

"You cannot overlook that it might be. Think what it would mean if it were," the countess urged. "Why, today Bartone will be at Whitehall voting. He is quite reformed, you know, and Kittridge says he has not missed a vote."

"That has nothing to do with this, Aunt Nettie," Mathilda said, with more force than necessary, as she turned away, wringing her hands. "I must return to the Hollows. Dannon and Mrs. Bertie will think I have deserted them."

"Write that you will return shortly and post the letter today so they can prepare for your homecoming," Lady Pennypiece advised. "Then fetch your bonnet. With or without you, I am calling at the Bartone residence. If I happen to fall on the stairs or from a chair as I search, the servants will find me"—she paused dramatically—"after a day or two."

Having no doubt that the viscount's servants would be outmanuevered by the countess if he were not at home, Mathilda decided reluctantly that it would be best if she accompanied her. "This is against all I hold," she repeated. "Won't you reconsider?"

"Here's your bonnet," the countess said, ignoring Mathilda's plea.

"I will not enter his house. What are you going to do if he is at home?" Mathilda asked, taking the hat angrily.

"We shall think that out only if it proves to be," Lady Pennypiece answered her lightly. "Wipe away those tears and come along. I mean to find that doll."

"Stand aside, I say," Lady Pennypiece ordered Green.

"But, my lady, Lord Bartone is not at home," the butler insisted.

"Then we shall await his return. Come, Mathilda," she called back to the coach. "The viscount is out and we must await him."

"Really, my lady, this is most awkward," Green protested.

"Silence. We shall wait in the library. You need not show us in—I know the way. Mathilda, come along," she commanded. "If we decide his lordship is too late in returning we shall see ourselves out. Go back to your duties," the countess ordered the butler haughtily.

"Yes, my lady," Green surrendered. What is one to do, after all, he thought. One cannot toss a countess out.

"I told you it would be simple," Lady Pennypiece told Mathilda. "Calm down. You will make me nervous. Let us search."

"Surely you are not going to go through his lordship's desk," Mathilda said, aghast as Lady Pennypiece pulled open a drawer.

"If he does not keep it locked, there can be nothing too personal in it."

"But you said the nursery. Where is it? How can we find our way there?"

"You underestimate me, Mathilda." Going to the door, she looked out. "No one is about. Follow me and remember, when challenged become insulted. The servants are never certain what to do in such a circumstance."

Looking to the right and left, ever watchful, Mathilda followed Lady Pennypiece to the third floor.

At the top of the stairs the old woman stopped and sat upon the last step. "Age is relentless," she noted acidly, catching her breath. Then she brightened. "I will remain here and keep watch. You go on. It is three doors down, then turn to your right. It is the second door to the left. If anyone happens upon you, tell them I felt faint and you went for help. Bring them here and I can assure such a fuss being raised that no one will ever question what we were doing up here. At least not until we are gone."

"Aunt Nettie, this is not the . . ."

"I have not come this far to leave without making an attempt. Now go."

Mathilda nervously tiptoed forward. *Three doors, turn right, and second door to the left,* she thought to herself. Second door . . . here it is. Gulping, she forced her hand to the door knob. The door swung open soundlessly, revealing the large, high-ceilinged nursery, bare but for dustcover-sheeted mounds. Two shapes resembled a cradle and a small child's bed. Small legs of a child-sized table and chairs peeped from beneath another cover. Shelves stood from the floor to beneath the tall windows on one wall. Walking to the windows, Mathilda gazed out and saw they overlooked the street in front of the house. She turned from them and circled the room. In one corner she spied an uncovered rocking horse and recalled Bartone speaking of one. It had to be the same one, she decided, seeing the tattered reins draped neatly across the neck. Drawn to it, her hand brushed across the smooth, worn wood, fingered the well-used reins. I can just see him on it, she thought, then shook herself. "Why can my thoughts not leave him?" she murmured aloud.

"Still regretting your misjudgment of Kittridge?" a masculine voice challenged.

All colour faded from Mathilda's cheeks at the words. Turning slowly, she faced him.

"Lady Bartone," the viscount said harshly, stepping uncertainly toward her. "An old man's wife, a rich widow," he said sarcastically. "What do you seek here?"

"You know what I have been searching for, my lord," she answered him with far greater calm than she felt, for the heavy odor of port indicated Bartone's condition.

"Was it necessary to drag good ol' Lady Netta along?" he asked, reaching out and pulling her roughly to him. "We could enjoy the day much more alone." His hand cupped her chin. "How'd you convince her to help you?" he asked, breathing into her face. "You do make a pretty thief, though."

"You have been drinking, my lord. I will go now."

"How?" he laughed, pulling her even closer. "Is this not better than a cold old man," he sneered, "or Kittridge?"

"I do not know," Mathilda said shakily, standing unresisting in his arms. "Neither man ever touched me."

"Never . . . touched . . . you," Bartone repeated. "You lie." He kissed her roughly.

"Never," she said shakily, when his lips released

hers. "And as for my being a thief—you know more of that than I. I could understand your seeking to deprive me, but the old servants—how could you?" she demanded, a tear running down her cheek.

Uncertainty softened the viscount's brazenness. He released his hold as confusion overwhelmed him.

"You are contemptible. Will you not even tell me why?"

Bartone stood unanswering.

"Are you too foxed to speak?" she cried. "Can you not see that justice demands they be taken care of?"

He shook his head, unable to comprehend; Mathilda took it for no. She gave the viscount a ringing slap across his face; tears streamed down her own. "I don't know what kind of man you are, but once I thought there was good in you. Lord Potters has done nothing but worry and fret over you. Why? What have you ever done but use him? How cruel can you be to pretend to take an interest in his work all these weeks? If there ever was any decency, there is none in you now. You'll die despised, at the bottom of a bottle of port," she sobbed, "and I don't care. No one will." Rushing past him, she ran from the room.

"Mathilda, whatever has happened?" Lady Pennypiece asked, rising from her stair-step seat. "Why are you crying?"

Mathilda brushed past her, unseeing. Escape was her only thought. Down the second flight and the first, flinging open the front door, she ran past the countess's coach and down the street.

Bartone, thought Lady Pennypiece, and she hurried down the stairs. She confronted Green as he closed the door, shaking his head at such happenings.

"Is Bartone in the house?" she demanded.

"Why, yes, but his lordship is not well and . . . and there were orders given he wished to see no one," Green tried to explain.

"You mean foxed," snapped Lady Pennypiece, angrier with herself than the unfortunate butler. "Where is Lady Bartone? Where is she?"

"Her ladyship ran right out the door, my lady."

"Well, open it—my coach," she said hopefully.

"No, my lady, I do not believe she took it," Green said, opening the door.

"Where is Lady Bartone?" Lady Pennypiece demanded of her coachman.

"My lady, she ran past."

"Ran past." Alarm appeared on the countess's face. "Open the door"—she shook her fist—"and find her."

Green sprang forward to open the door. "Calm yourself, my lady. Your age," he tried to soothe her.

Climbing into the coach, she paid no heed. The coach drove for some distance up, and an equal distance down, but there was no sign of Mathilda. Finally Lady Pennypiece tapped on the roof and called out. "Take me home."

In the nursery, Bartone was standing at the window when Lady Pennypiece departed. Mathilda's words echoed in condemnation. Worse, her tear-stained face would not fade from his mind.

The viscount had drunk heavily after seeing Mathilda at Mahew's ball, trying to ease the memory of how crushed she had been. Now her accusations, both in words and look, confused him. Turning from the window, he recalled how she had said, "I don't care."

With stumbling steps he went to the wooden horse he had seen her by when he had come into the nursery. He reached to touch where her hand had lain. Exhausted—physically and mentally—and further weakened by the drinking bout, he was overwhelmed by the truth of what he had done. Slowly, he sank to his knees, an arm thrown across the wooden horse's back, his head leaning against it. First one, then another tear fell upon the dust-filmed floor. Anguished sobs followed as Bartone faced himself squarely, completely, for the first time since his release by the French.

CHAPTER TWENTY-TWO

"Hollon, will you please take care of the hackney?" Mathilda asked tiredly when the huge butler opened the door.

"Lady Netta'll be most glad to see you. She's in the salon with . . . Mr. Kittridge. Hurry, now," he said, his relief apparent from his light scolding tone.

"Hollon, who are you talking . . . Mathilda." Kittridge strode forward anxiously. "What a fright you have given us. Mother will want to see you are unharmed." He took her hand and drew her forward. "She has been so distraught." Taking Mathilda into the small downstairs salon, he said, "See, she has returned."

"Oh, Mathilda, my dear." Lady Pennypiece rose. "I thought you were gone forever. Forgive me, please."

"I am the one who must be forgiven," Mathilda hugged her close. "But I had to get away. He said . . . I . . ."

"Don't explain—you needn't. I am a silly old fool to have thought . . ."

"You would never be that," Mathilda reprimanded her sternly. "It is I who have not been wise. You warned me."

"Mathilda, we have all made mistakes," Kittridge interposed.

She turned to him with a wry smile. "I can even forgive you, *Lord* Kittridge, when I think of my mistakes. Do not stand there looking so guilty." She extended her hand.

"Friends?" he asked, taking it.

She nodded. "I am in dire need of friends. While I was out I thought matters through very carefully. It will be best if I return to the Hollows now. Do you understand?" She looked to Lady Pennypiece.

"If I could keep you, I would," the countess answered, looking older than Mathilda had ever seen her. "But that would be what is best for me."

"I shall drive you tomorrow," Kittridge offered.

Mathilda shook her head. "Please arrange passage on the mailcoach for me. It is what I want."

"Will you insist on it?" he asked gently.

Nodding, she said, "Excuse me, please. I am very tired."

"I shall call to take you to the coachyard in the morn," Kittridge told her. "Sleep well."

"Thank you. Thank you both." She looked

slowly from one to the other, then fled before tears again came.

"Is his lordship at home, Green?" Lord Potters asked the butler. "He wasn't there for the vote today."

"Yes, my lord, but he is not receiving," Green answered, filled with worry and concern.

"Where is he?" Potters asked, handing over his hat and gloves.

"In the library, my lord. He has been there ever since Lady Bartone and Lady Pennypiece left this morn. We are quite concerned. We don't know what to do, my lord."

"Did they argue?"

"I don't know, my lord. But Lady Bartone was most distressed when she came down. Ran right out into the street without a word. And then Lady Pennypiece was very upset. I didn't know what to do."

Potters adjusted his spectacles nervously. "These matters are never as serious as they seem, Green. Lady Bartone is safely with Lady Pennypiece," he assured the worried butler. "I'll speak with his lordship. You needn't come with me."

"If you wish, my lord." Green remained at the door as the thin figure walked slowly to the library doors, knocked, and entered.

"Thank God," breathed Potters as he watched

the slow rise and fall of Bartone's chest as the viscount lay sleeping upon the sofa. Finding a flint, he lit a candle, then the lamps in the room. Shaking Bartone gently, he said, "Will. Will, wake up. It's Potts."

Awaking with a start, Bartone sat up, then fell back as he recognized Potters. He shook his head and rubbed it groggily. "Still speaking to me, Potts?"

"Only if you will consent to ride in my phaeton," the other returned.

A reluctant smile came to Bartone's lips. "I deserve a far worse fate than that."

"Why don't we decide that after we get you looking somewhat better," Potters answered, eyeing the unshaven, disheveled state of the other. "Frighten your own mother, you would," he said, tugging the bell cord and then pulling the viscount to his feet.

"Yes, my lords?" Green asked, entering anxiously.

"Water for his lordship to shave and bathe. Then a light supper for us both," Potters ordered, wrapping Bartone's arm across his shoulder and reaching under the other to support him. "Come along, Will," he told the viscount as the other leaned against him. "You may well have to do this for me one day. I want you to know exactly what to do."

* * *

"So you see, Potts," Bartone ended the telling of his last two encounters with Mathilda, "there is little hope for me with her."

"Let's get some food into you before we decide how hopeless the situation is. You are much improved already," the Baron quipped, taking in the simple black cutaway jacket and grey breeches. "I do wish you could show me the secret of your cravat, but then it would damage my image if I were to become a faultless dresser," he sighed. "Green is ready to serve, and you should be ready to do some justice to a meal."

Giving an uninterested shrug, Bartone followed. At supper Lord Potters chatted away, watching the viscount carefully, which ensured the latter ate, if only a little.

Over a single glass of port, the two settled into overstuffed, highbacked chairs before the library's ornately carved fireplace. A portrait of the late viscount gazed down at them with benign interest.

"What are you going to do now, Will?" Potters asked, breaking the silence that had fallen.

"Because of Angelique," he began, then glanced at Potters. "But then you don't know of that French beauty. There was a time I would have offered her as an excuse for my actions, but I see things far more clearly now."

"Would you tell me of her? She was in the Indies, was she not?"

"You could guess it all, Potts, and if anyone should know about her, it is you. What I have put you through demands that. But I can say, at last, that I no longer think of her with bitterness"—he paused—"or vengefulness." He dropped his head into his hands. "Tillie, what have I done to you?"

"This Angelique was responsible for your capture?" Potters asked quietly, deeply touched by his friend's anguish.

Bartone straightened and composed himself. "Yes. Because of her—no, because of my stupidity—I spent almost two years in the hands of the French. Oh, it could have been far worse. I almost led an entire company into their open arms. What a fool I was not to see her for what she was. I heard stories but just didn't . . ." He shook his head. "Isn't it ironic? I should have ignored what I heard about Tillie. There is a difference, though. With Angelique I followed my heedless heart; with Tillie I battled it. I realize now I only wanted to hurt her as I had been hurt, because I knew she had the power to wound me. I was so afraid . . . and I have hurt her so badly." Anguish filled his face. "Potts, do you think she would see me if I called?"

"Hollon has been told to prevent your entry," Lord Potters answered reluctantly.

"You've seen her this eve, then?"

"No, I spoke with Kittridge. Mathilda leaves for Bartone Hollows early in the morn. It is her wish.

He and Lady Pennypiece tried to dissuade her."

"Damme," Bartone cursed himself. "What am I to do? Should I try to see her before she goes?"

"Give her time. Give yourself time," Potters answered him. "I know little about these matters, but time does ease all things. Continue the work you've begun. See if your feeling for her remains. If she loves you, time will not matter, may even aid your cause." He paused awkwardly. "What can I say, Will? I . . ."

"Your being here is enough. I've failed everyone, Potts—you, Tillie, myself." He waved away the Baron's objection. "You could be right. Perhaps I must set myself aright and take care of all those who depend upon me first. Then Tillie could see I have truly changed. But I cannot let her go on believing the worst of me. I will write her a note . . ."

"But you will not be admitted," Potters told him.

"No, but you would. Will you take it to her for me?"

Potters debated with himself, then shrugged. "All right, Will."

"Thank you, my friend. I will ask her to see me a month from now. If she answers, I shall know there is a chance for me. For now, I will be content to try to learn what the reason behind the search for Doll in Red is. Oh, I haven't gone daft on you." He laughed at Potters's searching expression. "You see I've learned that Tillie has been searching for a doll, but I haven't the slightest idea why. Also she accused me of stealing away pensions from Bartone's old servants. I want to know the why of that also. I mean to write the solicitor handling the estate, and also we must find Nettles and set him upon the trail.

"Wait—Tillie came here—probably to search for the doll. I found her in the nursery. Let's go search it at once and I'll tell you all I know. I mean to find that doll!"

"My lord, there is a messenger from the Admiralty for you," Green said, as he intruded warily into the nursery.

"We'll see him in the library," Bartone ordered. "Wonder what this can be about. Have you heard of anything brewing?" he asked Potters as they left behind the disarray caused by their search and descended the three flights of stairs.

"You know I have little to do with the military. Have you no idea?" Potters asked.

Bartone shrugged and strode ahead, entering the library first. He accepted the message and read it through. "Are you to take an answer this eve?"

"I was ordered to return with you, my lord." The young officer shifted nervously. "St. Vincent's orders," he added hopefully. "A coach awaits us."

"I will be but a moment," Bartone said, waving dismissal to the messenger. He turned to Potters. "This must be of import. I'll be done with this in a moment," he told him as he sat and scrawled hurriedly across some paper. "Try to give it to Mathilda personally. According to the message, I should be gone a week, probably two, so tell her I may be delayed. I can't say more about it for now. If anyone asks after me, tell him I have gone to Bartone Hall." Hurriedly blotting the ink, he instructed Potters, "If you are unable to see Tillie, give it to Lady Pennypiece to hand on. I think she can be trusted to do so." He folded the note and sealed it. "Many thanks," Bartone said, handing it to the Baron and shaking his hand.

After seeing Bartone off, Lord Potters ordered his coachman to No. 31 Golden Square. Hollon returned to him in the entry after a prolonged wait. "Her ladyship, Lady Bartone, is not receiving this evening, but Lady Pennypiece said she would see you if the matter is urgent."

"Take me to her, then," Potters ordered, adjusting his spectacles.

He found Lady Pennypiece alone in the library.

"I had not thought to see you again this eve, Lord Potters. Is not the hour late?" Lady Pennypiece said, studying his lean figure through her quizzing glass.

"This call is not on my behalf, my lady. I have a

note which I have been asked to deliver to Lady Bartone personally," he answered.

"That is impossible. Mathilda was exhausted when she returned and is to bed. I will see that she receives the note," she told Potters, holding out her hand.

"Excuse my impertinence, my lady, but do I have your assurances that she will receive it? It is quite important."

"Young man, dare you question my integrity?"

"No, my lady, but it is of great import that it be given to Lady Bartone before she departs in the morn," he answered. Under the countess's steady gaze he surrendered the note to her outstretched hand.

"Is that all, my lord?" she asked, placing it in her skirt's inner pocket.

"Yes, my lady." Potters hesitated. "Do wish Lady Mathilda a pleasant trip for me."

"Thank you, my lord. I will be most happy to extend your thought. Now do forgive me, but I find myself fatigued."

"Good eve, then." The Baron bowed and withdrew with a breath of relief and a sigh of hope that her integrity was as sound as her haughtiness.

For some time after Lord Potters's leavetaking, Lady Pennypiece sat looking down at the missive he had given her. She had recognized Viscount Bartone's seal and was troubled. Feeling she had failed Mathilda so oft in the past, she was undecided about what to do. The note replaced in her pocket, she went to Mathilda's room and entered quietly, thinking she might be asleep.

"I am awake, Aunt Nettie," Mathilda spoke from her bed. "What is it you wish?"

The candle in Lady Pennypiece's hand lit the young woman's tear-stained face. "Is it because of Bartone that you weep?" she asked gently.

Her lips pressed into a thin line, Mathilda nodded.

"Do you not think it would be better to remain here a few days more? He may write or call," she offered.

Mathilda shook her head. "It would not matter. I have no wish to ever see him."

"But if he wrote explaining . . ."

With a violent shake of her head, Mathilda said, "It would not matter." Breaking into sobs, she turned her face into her pillow.

Deeply troubled by this, Lady Pennypiece reached out and patted her gently. "There now," she said, fighting back tears of her own, "the world will not end because of him. You shall see. Try to sleep, my dear. Good night." She leaned over and kissed her hair. Going to her own rooms, the countess withdrew the note and stared at it. She had promised to see it given, and yet . . . Fatigue jumbled her thoughts. Finally she sighed.

Mathilda has been hurt enough, she thought, and placed the note among her own personal papers.

"You shall need to be gone at least a month, if not longer," St. Vincent concluded. "Why the frown? Does the plan not suit you?"

"It is well thought out, but is there not someone else who could do this?" Bartone asked. "There is a personal matter that I would like to attend to."

"Unless it is a matter of life and death, the answer is no," St. Vincent answered bluntly. "Well?"

"It is not," Bartone returned reluctantly. "Have all the arrangements been made?"

St. Vincent nodded. "I knew you could be relied upon. We must know what Napoleon is about. Many believe the treaty will not last to the year's end. I cannot believe he would be so foolish as to do anything now. He needs a much longer time to rebuild. But we take no chances. Report to me immediately upon your return. Godspeed." The old admiral rose and reached out his hand.

Accepting it, Bartone restrained his objections. Surely Tillie would understand.

CHAPTER TWENTY-THREE

July had just begun when Mathilda returned to Bartone Hollows. August followed quickly on its heels as she struggled without success for a decision on what would be best for her and the three old servants.

It was a mid-August day when Dannon approached Mathilda and Mrs. Bertie as they sat in the shade of the ragged garden's trees, stitching infant wear for an impoverished family. "Madam, Mr. Petersbye wishes to speak with you. He awaits you in the salon."

The solicitor's name drew a frown from Mathilda. Was there to be more bad news? "You had better prepare tea," she told Mrs. Bertie. "We shall finish these after he has gone." Walking slowly toward the house, she wondered what he could want. She had not spoken with him since her return and dreaded doing so now, for every thought of the estate led to the viscount, and her heartache was still so tender. *If only Will had written, Mathilda thought, or if he had called upon me, as Aunt Nettie had suggested he might. But I must not think on it,* she told herself as she entered the cool corridor.

A moment's pause outside the salon door allowed her to smooth her hair and calm her emotions. Gripping the doorknob determinedly, she entered and greeted the solicitor. "How kind of you to call, Mr. Petersbye. Dannon will serve tea directly." She took a seat on one of the chairs and motioned for him to do likewise. "May I help you in some way?"

"I rather hope this news will help you, Lady Bartone," he answered eagerly. "As you know, it is now six months since Sir Bartone's death, and I thought it wise to review his instructions to see if there was some way to . . . to aid your situation."

"Were you able to find anything that would help?" Mathilda questioned, not daring to hope.

"Yes . . . and no," Petersbye answered. "I found the wording could perhaps be interpreted more loosely than I previously believed. It does not alter the matter greatly but may prove helpful." He looked to Mathilda, hopeful she understood his position.

"Yes, Mr. Petersbye?" she questioned, when he did not continue.

"Oh, well, my lady, I believe we could safely say that Sir Bartone intended that you be given the entire five hundred pounds at the end of the year, that ordinary expenses for the household be met by the estate." He smiled broadly, well pleased with his announcement.

"Is that all, Mr. Petersbye?"

"Why, I thought you would be pleased. I know it is not much, but . . ."

"Of course, it pleases me. And I thank you for taking the time and interest, Mr. Petersbye. I was hoping for . . . Well, I thank you for your effort," she smiled. "And here is Dannon with our tea. Has it not been warm of late . . ." Mathilda prattled on, her worry uneased.

Clumps of foam dappled the team's flanks and necks, and flies buzzed noisily over their drooping heads as they stood outside the Admiralty's office. The heat of this last week of August had proven almost too much with the speed the viscount had demanded of them, even for the short journey from the docks. Inside the building, limp collars and beaded brows showed the effect of the heat. Bartone himself paid no heed to his sweatsoaked clothing as he gave his report to St. Vincent.

"There is evidence enough. The shipbuilders are working at a frantic pace. Supplies are being stockpiled at Cherbourg and Le Havre." He concluded, "I have told you all I know."

"Excellent work, Bartone. Precise, detailed—just as I thought it would be," St. Vincent said, rising.

"We may need to call upon you again, but there is no further need at the moment. I know you are anxious to go."

"There are several matters demanding immediate attention," Bartone acknowledged. "One in particular I am most anxious about."

"Then you are bid good day," St. Vincent told him, shaking his hand.

On the street, the coachman, seeing Bartone's look as he approached, wondered what further journey awaited his exhausted team.

"To the nearest coachyard—a fresh team and on to London," the viscount ordered curtly. "You drive this time," he said, before stepping into the coach.

The trip to London, though fast by the day's standards, was endless to Bartone. Having been gone eight weeks, he felt a growing panic, wondering what Mathilda's answer had been and what her reaction was, since he had not been able to see her as promised or even to write of his delay.

He entered the city amid streets filled with the carts and wagons that brought the produce for London's teeming population. Noticeable by their absence on this hot afternoon were the *ton*—gone from the city to their cooler country seats. The viscount's house was one of the few still staffed among the titled whose presences were not required by the government or business needs.

Green held the door, greeting his master as if he had just returned from a leisurely afternoon jaunt, showing none of the relief he felt at Bartone's exhausted but healthy appearance.

"Bring me all correspondence at once," the viscount commanded, striding to his office. He flicked through the stack of calling cards, notes, and business letters. "Is this all?" he asked, dropping the last onto the desk top.

"Yes, my lord. Mr. Lynn took only those he knew to be pressing business matters. He has been most anxious for your return."

"Lay out fresh clothing and order my landau. Is Lynn in his office?"

"Yes, my lord."

Wordlessly, Bartone strode from the room and on to his secretary's office.

"My lord, you have returned," Lynn said with relief, looking up from his work to see who had entered. "I do hope you had a pleasant . . ."

"What is the trouble?" Bartone asked, dismissing the amenities.

"There has been an unusual amount of rain at the Hall—flooding. It has resulted in the loss of much of this year's crop. Some could be saved, according to Atler, your agent, but machinery must be purchased, and he also proposes immediate work on a system of dikes. I'm afraid your presence is demanded before much can be done. Also the Hall itself was damaged, and only you can decide what will be done there. And then there is the problem of . . ."

"Never mind, Lynn. Complete a report, with any papers needing my signature. I must go out briefly. When I return, we will go over matters and arrange to go to the Hall and take care of it all. See all is arranged by the time I return."

Freshened and dressed in dry clothing, the viscount stepped into his landau and ordered his driver to No. 31 Golden Square. Arriving there, he did not even bother to descend, seeing the boarded windows and the knocker removed. There was nothing to do but try Kittridge's bachelor apartments on Chesterfield Street and hope something could be learned.

From the Chesterfield address he was directed to White's. Kittridge was leaving the club just as Bartone's landau halted before it. "May I walk with you?" he asked as he stepped down.

Kittridge nodded, and Bartone fell into step with him. "Rumour has it you have been to France," he noted.

"Some should be careful of what they hear or repeat," Bartone answered tonelessly. He halted. "It is a personal matter I must speak with you about. Has your mother gone to Pennywise?"

"Yes, she prefers to summer there," Kittridge answered, stepping forward once more.

"Is Mathilda with her?"

"Lady Bartone?"

The viscount took hold of Kittridge's arm, then released it. "You have no reason to think well of me, but believe this—I mean Mathilda no harm. I only wish to help her, even if she refuses to see me," he spoke earnestly.

"She is not with mother—refused to come to Pennywise."

"Do you know if she is well?" Bartone's anxiety showed in his looks as much as in his words.

"I believe so. She has written me, but has asked that I not come to the Hollows," Kittridge offered.

"Do you know why she was searching for Doll in Red?"

The other shook his head. "I heard mention of it when Mathilda first arrived but nothing since."

Motioning for his coachman to drive forward, Bartone thanked Kittridge and shook his hand before leaping into the landau and ordering its return to his home.

He may yet be the man for her, Kittridge thought, watching the departing carriage. Not a word to say about eight weeks in France. Many a man would have bragged. He seemed only concerned for Mathilda. Hopefully Mother will see it also, he thought, thinking of the opinion she had voiced of Bartone after Mathilda's departure.

* * *

Three days later, having attended to the most pressing needs Lynn presented and having made arrangements to meet him at Bartone Hall, Viscount Bartone paced impatiently in a small receiving salon at Pennywise, waiting to learn if Lady Pennypiece would see him. His forbearance at being made to wait was severely tested; only the importance of learning something which could help Mathilda kept him there.

"Her ladyship will see you now, my lord," Hollon told the viscount at last. "Follow me." He proceeded through the wide corridors with their alternate bands of frieze work and rich paneling to a shaded veranda, where Lady Pennypiece sat waiting. Her look was one of a judge about to dispose of a despised criminal.

"My lady, I thank you for seeing me." Bartone bowed lowly. "Let me assure you I seek only to learn of a way in which I can help Mathilda." He came quickly to his point. "I believe she was desperately searching for a doll known as Doll in Red, and I wish to know why."

"So it was you who were asking questions, and I thought it was my nuisance of a sister. But why ask me," the countess questioned haughtily, "when you know the truth of the matter?"

"But I do not know it fully, my lady. I know Mathilda thinks I do, but I know nothing that will explain the mystery to me. Please tell me what you know," he pleaded.

"What will you do if I consent to do so?" she asked.

"I shall do whatever is in my power to help Mathilda," Bartone answered simply. "There was no answer to the note I had written. I can do no more than hope to aid her cause if help is needed. Somehow I feel it is." He looked unwaveringly at Lady Pennypiece. "My . . . faults have cost me her love. Would you deny me the little I seek to do?"

His words rang true; his eyes blazed with anguish. Lady Pennypiece raised her hand to her breast, recalling the note she had chosen to ignore. "She will not accept your help; she has refused everyone's," she said, trying to fob him off.

"What troubles her? Why the search for the doll?" he asked again.

His intensity appealed to the countess. Her guilt at having failed to do as she had promised prompted her answer. "My brother, God rest his soul, put a stipulation in his will that Mathilda was to receive only five hundred pounds from his estate unless she handed the doll—Doll in Red—over to his solicitor within a year."

"And if she does not?"

"All is to go to you."

"To me! Oh, God, no wonder . . . But I will see the solicitor at once and refuse . . ."

"You know that is impossible. She would not accept it from you even if you tried. No, in her last letter Mathilda insisted she would find work as a governess. Finding the doll is the only solution, and I have gone over every possible place it could be. I believe it no longer exists and cannot fathom why Howard put such a stipulation in his will."

With Mathilda's tear-stained, tormented face before him, Bartone swore, "Describe the doll to me. If it can be found, I will do it."

CHAPTER TWENTY-FOUR

"What have you there?" Mrs. Bertie asked Dannon.

"It was sent from London," he answered, turning the box over and over. "By special coach—for Madam."

"Perhaps it is something from Lady Pennypiece," Mrs. Bertie said hopefully. "Something to cheer her. Put it in her room. Miss should be returning soon, for she was only taking a basket of bread and cheese to the Caylors."

With Petersbye's announcement, Mathilda had been freed to resume her efforts among the poor, widowed, and orphaned of Horley. These occupied an increasing amount of her time as August heat cooled into September. No matter how much she did, however, it never succeeded in turning her thoughts from Bartone for long. In the week just past she had received a letter from Kittridge and had been surprised to see, interspersed between his lively news and tales of the latest *on dits,* praise of the viscount—word of a secret journey to France, of his attention to his estate, and increased involvement in Parliament. She had read it greedily, her heart thirsting for any word after months of silence, and was vastly relieved to learn that Bartone was no longer drowning himself in port.

All of this filled Mathilda's thoughts as she returned to her room and saw the plainly wrapped box.

A quick examination did not reveal the sender, and with shaking hands she removed the bindings and slowly undid it. Opening the lip carefully, she tossed the packing filler aside and saw a second, smaller box. With it in hand, she sat upon her bed. Tissue greeted her eyes as she lifted its lid. With trembling fingers she pulled that aside. Her eyes widened at the sight of the red lace flounces of the elegant court dress, the delicate features of the china face. A small card lay beside the doll—from Viscount Bartone.

What does this mean? Mathilda pondered, holding his card in her hand. She rose and paced, stopping to gaze at the doll each time her steps neared the bed. The dainty figure only stared vacantly, unanswering. So like Doll in Red, Mathilda thought, yet not it. Why had it been sent?

He mocks me, her tormented mind answered at last. Cradling the doll in her hands, Mathilda thought how he must have held it.

"Why, miss, tears? Why are you crying?" Mrs. Bertie exclaimed, thinking to find her mistress smiling over a gift. "The doll—has someone found the doll?" she asked, seeing the red skirts.

Mathilda wiped her eyes with the back of her hand. "No," she sniffled. "It is not Doll in Red. Only a cruel joke."

"But who would . . ." The housekeeper's words ended as she saw the calling card in the empty box.

"Not another one," Lord Potters exclaimed, entering Bartone's office during the first week of October.

"This one resembles even more closely the description Lady Pennypiece gave me. I can only hope it is the one," the viscount said, looking at the doll standing at one side of his desk. "Until I find the right one, nothing will stop me. Nettles has two men helping him in the search. I don't care if they must examine every shop in England."

"When will you know you have found the right one?" Potters asked.

"Mathilda has not written yet, but I am certain she will if I send Doll in Red."

"So she has not written—and still you go on," Potters said, taking a seat.

"It was foolish of me to think she would take pity, or care for me still. I cannot blame her. But enough of this." Bartone tried to dismiss it lightly.

"Have we gained any more support in the Commons?"

"Wilberforce believes it will still be two or three years before final success can be achieved, but there are inroads. We must keep to it. What of Napoleon?" the baron asked, removing his spectacles and rubbing his eyes.

"The general news is not promising. I fear there will be war again in less than a year. There has been too much talk of our disbanding the army. Our work is really beginning now that almost everyone has returned to town. When Parliament convenes next week, we shall have little rest."

"Which is why we should relax now. Come with me to Alvenly's soiree. There will be ladies enough to make it interesting," Potters urged.

Bartone shook his head. "There are too many matters here." He motioned at the papers covering his desk. "I am still paying for lost time. Go on—perhaps the next time," he said, and returned to his work.

With a last look at the doll, and replacing his spectacles, Potters decided the time had come to approach Lady Pennypiece. He could not believe Lady Mathilda to be so unfeeling toward his friend or so unforgiving. The answer to her silence, he felt, would be found with the countess if anywhere.

* * *

"Who was that, Dannon?" Mathilda asked, having heard the doors close as she came from the library.

"Another package, madam," he answered reluctantly, looking at the plain wrapping—exactly like the one which had brought the dolls in September and October.

"Open it," she ordered, turning ashen.

His old hands firmly removed the outer wrapping, opened the box, and revealed the layer of packing.

"Go on," Mathilda said when he glanced at her.

The second lid, once raised, revealed a doll, dressed in red.

"It is from Lord Bartone," Dannon said, looking at the calling card placed next to the doll.

"Place it with the others," Mathilda choked out despite the large lump in her throat. "I am going out."

"Your cloak, madam. Let me bring it for you," Dannon called after her, but Mathilda was already through the doors and into the damp cold of the November day.

A cold slush covered London with a deep chill. At No. 31 Golden Square Lord Kittridge angrily confronted his mother.

"It has been four months since Bartone came to you and still you do nothing."

"This constant badgering is too much," Lady

Pennypiece retorted. "When will you and Lord Potters cease this . . . crusade?"

"When you come to your senses. Ever since you returned from Pennywise you have been sitting in this house sulking. If you do not write to Mathilda and urge her to write Bartone, I shall," he threatened. "Bartone has proven himself. Despite all the time he now gives to causes of all sorts, he still worries constantly about her. I know Mathilda cares for him. Why must they both be made to suffer?"

Lady Pennypiece shrank into old age before his eyes. Fear and doubt assailed her.

"Mother, what is it? Write to Mathilda. Tell her to come. Tell her to write to the viscount. That is all I ask," he urged.

"Why do you champion Bartone?" she asked, averting her eyes.

"It is not Bartone I think of but Mathilda, and so must you. I don't care what has happened—what you fear—but I do know you can convince her he is sincere. . . . Why, you are crying." Kittridge dropped to one knee before his mother and took her hands.

"I have done . . . done the unpardonable," she told him. "Before Mathilda left, Lord Potters brought a note written by the viscount for her and I . . . I never gave it to her. She will never forgive me once she learns of it. Oh, I cannot bear to have Mathilda hate me."

"You know she would never do that."

Lady Pennypiece straightened herself and wiped the last tear away. "I never thought I could live too long," she said tiredly, "or act so foolishly. I must do what is best for Mathilda. Will she believe I never thought to harm her?"

Kittridge held her close. "You have no need to fear that."

"My son is amazing," she said, "despite his mother. I shall write immediately. No, send for Bartone and I shall tell him what I have done and give him a letter to carry to Mathilda."

"He has already left for Bartone Hall and won't return till January. I spoke with him the last day of Parliament," he explained. "But that could be best," he offered, a plan coming to his mind. "I shall take you to Pennywise and then travel on to Horley and spend some time at Bartone Hollows. I can learn Mathilda's feelings and return to Pennywise, and we should return to London about the same time Barton is due. Let us make no mistake this time." He smiled at his mother. "All will be well, despite the lack of Doll in Red."

CHAPTER TWENTY-FIVE

"The trunk!" exploded from Viscount Bartone.

"Quiet, Will. You want people to think you've gone mad?" Lord Potters warned his friend. "One does not shout about trunks in the middle of an operatic scene."

"Why didn't I think of it before? Let's go." Bartone rose from his seat and marched from the box.

Potters followed. "Are you headed for Bedlam? What are you raving about?"

"I'll tell you as we go," the viscount answered, accepting his hat and cloak from the page and walking on. Inside the coach he could scarcely contain his eagerness. "The trunk Bartone sent may have the doll in it. There was a letter sent with it, but it must have been lost long ago. I never have come across it."

"What will you do when you find the trunk? What if your housekeeper has seen fit to toss it out?"

"That couldn't be," Bartone swore. "I must take

it to Mathilda. It may be the chance to speak with her I have been seeking."

His staff were comfortably settled in their rooms when Bartone and Potters burst into the house. "Green!" Bartone shouted, pulling the bell cord.

Hastily donning a robe and slippers, Green ran to see what had caused so early a return. "My lord, you said we need not await your return . . ."

"Never mind that. Now, Green, do you recall the trunk that was in my office when I returned last spring from the Indies? The one that Sir Bartone had sent?"

Green scratched his head thoughtfully. "Ah, the one you ordered sent to the attics," he recalled at last.

"Yes. Get dressed, rouse the others, and search for it now. I want it found," Bartone commanded. "It is very important."

"Now, my lord? But it is . . . Yes, my lord," he ended, knowing what the viscount's present look meant. "At once."

An hour later a dusty, disheveled Green stepped into the library followed by two footmen, similarly unkempt, carrying a dusty, battered trunk.

"Will that be all, my lord?" he asked tiredly, after dismissing the footmen.

"Arrange for my landau to be ready to depart at first light. Send someone ahead to have teams ready for me. I travel to Horley. Pack clothing for seven days at the least."

"Yes, my lord," Green bowed, inwardly sighing.

"And have this trunk put in the landau when it comes, along with my baggage. I wish only a driver, and order him warmly dressed."

"Will, you can't mean to travel in this weather," Potters objected. "The December snows have melted and the roads are wretched."

"Would you have me wait until May? No. Mathilda was given one year. That leaves her only one month. I must go now."

"But you don't know that the doll is in the trunk."

"And I will not from the looks of this lock," Bartone answered, fingering the large metal lump.

"She may not receive you," Potters warned.

"That does not matter. If necessary I will leave the trunk on her doorstep," the viscount answered. "There is something I would like you to do . . ."

"I am not going with you," Potters objected.

"No, no. I need you to explain to Kittridge that I shall call upon him as soon as I return. He sent a message to the Hall that I should see him as soon as I returned, but I find he has been delayed himself. I think he will understand my impatience. Wish me well, good friend."

Potters reached out, clasping Bartone's hand. "Godspeed."

* * *

"Who can that be?" Mrs. Bertie asked, looking up from her work as the sounds of a coach and four reached her ears.

"Has that Lord Kittridge come back?" she asked Dannon, who was peering out the window.

"Whoever it is has traveled far," he answered, noting the spattered team and mud-coated landau. "Poor way to travel in this weather," he said, scorning the light carriage. "They must be frozen through. I best go down."

The knocker was pounding by the time Dannon reached the front doors. Pulling them open, he greeted the traveler. "Step inside. You must be near frozen."

Unwrapping the muffler about his face, Bartone nodded agreement. "Is Lady Bartone at home?" he asked.

"You," Dannon said, breaking the first rule of in-service by showing his surprise and alarm. "My lord," he collected himself. "I do not believe you are welcome in this house," he said stiffly.

"Will you tell Lady Bartone that it is important that I speak with her?" the viscount persisted.

"Her ladyship is resting."

"Please tell her I will return this eve, Dannon."

The use of his name caused the butler's brows to raise. "I cannot say that Lady Bartone will receive you, Lord Bartone."

"How is she?" he asked.

"In good health, my lord," Dannon answered coldly. Giving a bow, he opened the door.

Curiosity had brought Mrs. Bertie down the stairs. "Who was it? Are they not staying?"

"That was Viscount Bartone asking to see madam as bold as you please," Dammon told her.

"Why? Oh, after all those dolls. What can he want?" Mrs. Bertie fretted.

"He asked how madam was and said he would return this eve. I told him he would not be seen."

"What are we going to do? Miss will be terribly upset." Mrs. Bertie wrung her hands and looked to see if her husband had a ready answer.

"We must tell madam he has called," the old butler said. "I doubt he will go without seeing her. There is that look of Bartone stubbornness about him."

"Then I'll get me hat pin. We'll see how he likes a taste o' it," Mrs. Bertie bristled, thinking of the swordlike anchor for hats.

"Best have the two settle things between themselves," Dannon remonstrated. "But we can stay close in case madam needs us," he amended after a scathing glance from his wife.

"Kittridge, you've returned at last. Rather tardy, aren't you? Parliament opens tomorrow," Lord Potters said, shaking the other's hand.

"The roads are almost impassable. Didn't think we'd ever reach London and must take care with mother's age, you know. Tell me, has Bartone been here long?" Kittridge asked anxiously.

"Long returned and gone again," Potters laughed. "He asked me to tell you he will call upon you as soon as he returns. Tried to persuade him to wait, but he wouldn't hear of it. Love and all that, you know," Potters laughed again.

"Love? He has gone to the Hollows?" Kittridge asked in surprise.

"Seems a trunk had been sent to Will by Old Bartone with instructions that it was to be returned to his widow. One night not more than a week past, while we were at Covent Gardens, Will jumps up and shouts 'the trunk.' Insisted we go right to his house and search for it. The next day he was off to Horley with it."

Kittridge laughed softly. "The best-laid plans," he explained, "are oft improved upon by not being used. This should relieve Mother. Let us go to White's and drink a toast to the pair."

"You think Lady Mathilda will see him, then?" Potters asked hopefully.

"Oh, I think Lady Mathilda will marry him," Kittridge answered with a smile.

In Bartone Hollows the matter did not appear so promising.

"Lady Bartone will not see you, my lord. I cannot make it clearer. She is adamant in that decision," Dannon told a bristling Viscount Bartone for the third time.

"Have you explained . . ."

"Exactly as you instructed, my lord. Her ladyship still refuses," the butler told him.

"Make it clear to Lady Bartone that I have with me a trunk sent to me by Sir Bartone with instructions to return it to her personally. I am bound by his wish." He paused for a moment, striving to control his irritation. "I shall call one last time in the morn. Reason with her, Dannon. It is to her best interests that she see me and accept the trunk. And also to yours," Bartone said before stalking out of the house.

Back at the simple inn, the viscount retired to his room and paced before the fireplace. What would he do if Mathilda still refused to see him in the morn?

CHAPTER TWENTY-SIX

"Madam, the trunk may contain the doll," Dannon appealed to Mathilda. "Perhaps he has repented and wishes to make amends for his treatment of you. He said this morn would be the last time he would offer it to you," he ended.

"Please see him, miss," Mrs. Bertie entreated. "You need not even speak with him. We shall be at your side."

"If ye wish, milady, I'll bring me old blunderbuss to the house," Old Jerry offered.

Mathilda smiled warmly at him, shaking her head. "That will not be necessary. I shall see him as you wish. But I have no desire to speak with him."

"That shall be made clear to him, madam," Dannon told her. "Where will you wish to receive his lordship?"

"The library will be the most suitable place, I suppose. See that a fire is laid there and call me before admitting him to the house," Mathilda told them. "I shall be in my room."

"Very good, madam." Dannon bowed, hopeful that they were right in persuading Madame to do this.

"Do you really think there is a chance it be in it?" Old Jerry asked when Mathilda was gone.

"We won't know until it is opened," Dannon told him. "I pray it is not a hoax on the part of his lordship. Let us hope for the best."

"I'm still bringing my hat pin," Mrs. Bertie said obstinately. "His lordship will mind his manners with miss."

An early-morning ride on one of the inn's better mounts did nothing to ease Lord Bartone's mind. Sitting before the fireplace of the inn's common room, he watched the flickering of the smoky fire and awaited time's slow passage for a more reasonable hour. At ten he could stay his impatience no longer.

"Ready the teams," he commanded his coachman. "Hire someone to help with the trunk. Put it in the landau and call me when you are ready."

In a half hour they were on the road to the Hollows. Brilliant sunlight danced across the ice-covered puddles, causing them to glitter like crown jewels. The air was crisp and clear, promising improved weather and lifting Bartone's spirits.

When the coach halted before the Hollows, Bartone adjusted his cravat, wishing the inn had had at least one full-length looking glass. Bracing himself, he assumed a deceptively bland expression and stepped nonchalantly from the coach. After ordering the men the coachman had hired to bring the trunk, he strode up the steps and dropped the heavy knocker once.

It was an eternity's minute before Dannon opened the door. "Madam has consented to see you, my lord," he announced stiffly. "But she requested that you not speak directly to her." Turning, he led the way to the library.

Swallowing, Bartone followed Dannon, motioning the men with the trunk to do the same.

Mathilda stood before the fireplace in a gown of violet wool, the coloring enhancing the paleness of her cheeks. Two bright spots flared upon them at the sight of Bartone before she lowered her eyes from his searching gaze.

After Dannon had directed the placing of the trunk before Mathilda, Bartone dismissed the men, telling them to have his coachman take them to the inn and then return for him. This done, he stepped toward the trunk, halted only a few feet from it, and stared at Mathilda, longing to reach out and take her in his arms.

"Hruumph." Dannon cleared his throat and motioned for Bartone to step back.

"I feel I owe you many apologies, my lady," the viscount spoke to Mathilda, ignoring Dannon. "Let me extend one for the tardy return of this trunk. It was but eight days past that I recalled its existence. You can see it is locked—just as it was when it was delivered to my house in London. No key was sent with it." With his eyes he begged Mathilda to speak to him.

"His lordship kept some keys in his desk, madam," Dannon offered. "Would you wish me to see if I can locate the proper one for the trunk?"

Mathilda nodded.

"My lord, it is unfortunate that you ordered your coach to leave. You shall now have to wait at the door until it returns," Dannon told the viscount.

"I will go when I have seen what is in the trunk," Bartone answered, his posture indicating he would not be moved.

"It is all right," Mathilda said as Old Jerry moved toward the viscount. "He may see what it contains. Bring that ring of keys from the right-hand drawer, Dannon." She raised her eyes to Bartone's. His lordship's behaviour baffled her. Each month he had sent a different doll, as if taunting her, and now his eyes spoke to her with love.

Returning with the keys, Dannon knelt before the trunk and began trying them, one after another. As key after key failed to open the lock, all drew closer and closer about the trunk. At last only one key remained. Slowly Dannon eased it into the lock. They all held their breath as he turned it. Mrs. Bertie gasped as a loud click announced the lock's release.

Dannon slowly looked to Mathilda, who nodded, and he eased the lock off and slowly opened the lid. A layer of straw startled everyone.

"Fetch a blanket," Mathilda ordered. "I'll not have the room straw-strewn like a stable."

The straw was removed to the blanket and four chests of differing sizes were revealed. Dannon removed one and handed it to his mistress. All stood as she warily opened it.

"Oh, miss," exclaimed Mrs. Bertie at the sight of a beautiful pearl necklace and a chain of diamonds within. "You'll have no more worries."

"Look what the others contain," Bartone urged her, still hoping to see the long-sought doll.

Mrs. Bertie took the first chest, closing its lid, and Dannon handed the second to Mathilda.

This one she opened quickly. A rolled parchment met her eyes.

"May I?" Bartone asked, reaching for it.

Forgetting her reluctance, Mathilda held the chest forward.

Taking the parchment out and unrolling it, the viscount glanced over it, reading swiftly. "This is a deed to a house in London, near Mayfair," he said returning the parchment to her hand.

This Mathilda also handed on to Mrs. Bertie and accepted the third and smallest chest. It contained only a single letter, addressed to her in Sir Bartone's shaky hand. Taking it out, she set the chest back in the trunk.

"Only one remains," Dannon noted. "Will you open it, madam?" he asked as he removed it.

"I wish you to open it," she told him, still clutching the letter.

All looked on in silence as he pried open the lid. "Doll in Red," he said. "It is exactly as it is in the portrait, madam." He looked at Bartone. "We must thank you, my lord."

"Yes, we must," Mathilda added hesitantly. "I do not know what else to say."

"Read the letter, Mathilda," Bartone urged her, stepping around the trunk to her side.

She walked to the sofa and sat. Biting her lip, she opened the letter with trembling hands. All four watched as she read the single page. When she reached the last word, the letter fluttered from her hand to the floor as she buried her face in her hands and broke into sobs.

Bartone bounded to her side, never realizing Dannon's hold upon his wife's arm saved his person from a sudden and painful abuse. With one arm holding Mathilda close, Bartone picked the letter up and read. It was brief.

My dearest Tillie,

It is my fondest wish that your search has led you to my young cousin, Viscount Bartone, and that your reading this now finds a fondness between you both. It is my desire that you wed him. Barring that possibility, I hope you find the accompanying jewels and house ample proof of my affection and esteem.

The short note ended with Bartone's signature.

While the viscount was reading, Dannon, seeing how matters stood, shepherded Old Jerry and his reluctant wife from the scene, closing the doors behind them.

"Dear, dear Tillie, will you ever let me make up for all I have done? I love you so," Bartone told her, dropping the letter.

Drawing back, she attempted to wipe her eyes. "Love," she sniffled. "How can you torment me so?"

Bartone took her face gently in both his hands. "I swear I do," he told her. "Look and you shall see it is true. Forgive me for all I have done."

Fear and disbelief turned to joy as Mathilda studied his face and saw the truth in his eyes. Tears of joy flowed as she embraced him.

They kissed lingeringly, with a desire long despaired of. Reluctantly, Bartone held her from him. "I must explain, Tillie."

"I wish only to know if you are certain this time. I could not stand to lose you."

He kissed her fingers one by one. "Did you think it mad of me to send the dolls?" he asked.

"Worse. I thought you were taunting me," she answered.

"How could you, after my note?" he asked, appalled at what she must have felt. "Oh, Tillie, I have been such a fool."

"My lord . . ." she began.

"Will," he interrupted her, "or 'Willful' if you prefer." He laughed at her puzzlement. "My name," he explained. "No, do not speak." The viscount gripped her hand. "You must know why I was so horrid to you. There must never be any doubt in your mind of my love." With halting words he spoke of Angelique and her betrayal, of his bitterness, of Nettles's investigation, and finally of his love. "When you did not answer the note I had Potters take to Lady Pennypiece, I almost lost hope." He gazed at her lovingly. "I do hope she will be reconciled to our marrying, for I know you care for her. And I can even manage my jealousy of Kittridge, if you will swear it is I alone you love."

"You know it is only you," Mathilda replied, then paused as she tried to remember the note he mentioned. Finally she recalled that brief conversation with Lady Pennypiece the night before she left London. That is what Kitt meant, she thought.

Aunt Nettie did not give me the note because I said I would never accept it. The poor dear, to think she has worried over it all this time.

"What are you thinking, my love?" Bartone asked, his hand brushing her cheek.

She shook her head. He need never know. They were together now and that was what mattered.

"Will you marry me?" he asked, suddenly alarmed.

"Are you certain that is what you wish? I did marry Sir Bartone for the security he could give me," she admitted.

"I don't care why you married him. I love you so." Bartone crushed her to him. "Say you will."

"You know I will."

"When?"

"As soon as Aunt Nettie can arrange a small wedding," Mathilda answered with a wide smile.

"Lady Pennypiece?" The viscount rolled his eyes.

"But think, we shall have the most unusual wedding in all London. I mean to give her free rein."

"I shall gladly suffer anything," Bartone answered. "Even Potts driving our carriage," and he demonstrated his willingness with no complaint from Mathilda.

Outside the library's doors, Mrs. Bertie frowned. "They have become frightfully quiet. We had better see . . ."

"No, we had better not see," said her husband. "Instead turn your mind to preparing a hearty meal. Something tells me we shall have a very happy and a very hungry mistress, to say nothing of the viscount. Nothing like passion to make appetites hearty." Dannon gave Mrs. Bertie's bottom a sound pat.

"'Pon my soul, sir," she exclaimed, then kissed his cheek and gave him a hug. "May they be blessed with as many years together as we."